"She walked slowly toward us. There seemed to be a silence around her, as there would be for a heroine making her first entrance in a stage play.... The long silver chain she wore swung to the rhythm of her walk.... She seemed so incredibly lovely to me that when she gave me her hand, looking directly into my eyes and saying, 'Ah?', I felt a little movement of pain in my heart."

Forbidden Fires

by Margaret Anderson

Edited and with an Introduction by Mathilda Hills

THE NAIAD PRESS, INC.
1996

Printed in the United States of America on acid-free paper
First Edition

Copy Editor: Judy Eda
Cover designer: Bonnie Liss (Phoenix Graphics)
Typesetter: Sandi Stancil

The picture of Margaret Anderson, Paris, c. 1930 on page 18, the picture of
Solita Solano, Paris, 1927 on page 128, and the picture of Jane Heap,
Paris, 1927 on page 124, all by Berenice Abbott, are reproduced with the
permission of Commerce Graphics Ltd., Inc.

Library of Congress Cataloging-in-Publication Data

Anderson, Margaret C.
    Forbidden fires / by Margaret Anderson : edited and introduction
by Mathilda Hills.
        p.   cm.
    ISBN 1-56280-123-6
    1. Lesbians—Fiction. I. Hills, Mathilda M. II. Title.
PS3501.N2497F6   1996
813'.52—dc20   95-25876
                                                             CIP

About the Editor

Mathilda M. Hills was born in Salem, Massachusetts. She received the B.A. from Radcliffe College and attended the Royal Academy of Dramatic Art. After a brief career Off-Broadway, she turned to teaching, and in 1970 earned the Ph.D. from Duke University. She is currently an Associate Professor of English and Women's Studies at the University of Rhode Island, where she teaches Shakespeare and Expatriate Women Writers in Paris.

CONTENTS

Acknowledgments

First and foremost I acknowledge the loving care taken by the late Elizabeth Jenks Clark in preserving the papers of her friend Margaret Anderson and the many photographs reproduced here. As I attempt to make clear in the Postscript, without Elizabeth Clark's efforts, there would be no book.

I am especially grateful to the late Michael Currer-Briggs, a dedicated "pupil" in Jane Heap's London Gurdjieff group, for his work preserving Margaret Anderson manuscripts and for sharing important biographical information with me.

Thanks to the extraordinary kindness of Jane Purse, I was able to examine over several days her vast, lovingly preserved collection of Jane Heap treasures, originally preserved by Florence E. Reynolds and by her niece, Florence Treseder. Since that visit the University of Delaware has acquired the material as the Florence E. Reynolds Collection, and an edition of Jane Heap's letters, edited by Holly Baggett, is in preparation for the New York University Press.

Margaret Anderson's sister Lois Anderson Karinsky, Angèle B. Levesque, Kathryn Hulme, Gertrude Macy, Janet Flanner, Jacqueline Ingram Porter, Florence Codman and Chloe Champcommunal contributed vivid memories of Margaret Anderson and her circle and insights into a now-past culture.

Thanks to the hospitality of Marcelle Simon, Margaret Anderson's friend in Le Cannet, I have beautiful memories of the Avenue Victoria's spectacular setting above the Mediterranean as well as the delicious cuisine of the Côte d'Azur. With her as my guide I was able to visit the grave site of Margaret Anderson, Georgette Leblanc and Monique Serrure.

Behind the scenes are the many librarians, past and present, whose labors and many kindnesses enabled me to benefit from our heritage. I particularly want to thank librarians in Interlibrary Loan at the University of Rhode Island and the guardians of manuscripts at the Berg Collection in the New York Public Library, the Flanner-Solano Collection in the Library of Congress, the Harry Ransom Humanities Research Center of the University of Texas at Austin, the Beinecke Library at Yale University, the Golda Meir Library of the University of Wisconsin-Milwaukee, and the Van Volkenburg-Brown Collection, Special Collections, the Library at the University of Michigan. A Newberry Library Fellowship enabled me to do extensive research on the Chicago period of *The Little Review.*

The University of Rhode Island Foundation generously funded my initial research for a projected biography of Margaret Anderson, and a sabbatical leave provided me with the time for further research and writing. Professor Lois A. Cuddy, with her uncommon generosity of mind, arranged for me to read a paper on Margaret Anderson at her house, inviting friends and colleagues in English and Women's Studies. Versions of that paper were presented at conferences on the thirties in Youngstown, Ohio, and on twentieth-century literature in Louisville, Kentucky, where I benefited from the encouragement and advice of Edward Burns and Mary Lynn Broe.

Permission was kindly granted by Hélène Pardo of Commerce Graphics to reproduce three Berenice Abbott portraits, by George Clark and Jane Burns to quote Jane Heap, and by Bertha Harris and Alfred Kazin to quote from their writings. My enthusiastic, telecommunicative publisher, Barbara Grier, arranged permission to quote Jeannette Foster.

Coburn Britton, the publisher of Margaret Anderson's three-volume autobiography in 1969, contributed in no small way to the preservation of her memory and to the happiness of her last years.

I am grateful for the loyal support of my sister, Alicia H. Moore, in this endeavor, and that of my friends Ann A. Zener, Joseph S. Clark, Jr., Merloyd Ludington and Rebecca Dexter.

Introduction

Tap, tap, tap, TAP. Tap, tap, tap, tap, tap, TAP. . . . *The sound of a typewriter broke the fragrant, pre-dawn silence of a Mediterranean hillside. Margaret Anderson was writing a novel. The legendary editor of* The Little Review *had returned to live in Le Cannet after the death of her last great love, Dorothy Caruso, and this revision of a long-ago romance would give her a start on a new life, here in France where she had experienced her greatest joys and her first great sorrow.*

Mrs. Anderson and Margaret (standing, center), Jean (seated, left) and Lois (seated, right), Youngstown, Ohio, 1899.

Margaret Carolyn Anderson was born in 1886 in Indianapolis, Indiana, a city of wide, tree-lined boulevards, and spent her youth in Youngstown, Ohio, then a city of vast, grimy steel mills. There her father, Arthur Aubrey Anderson, of Scottish and Dutch descent, managed the combined vast utilities and street

1

railway system. Her mother, Jessie Shortridge, of Kokomo, Indiana, came from a distinguished family, boasting a Civil War governor. A trolley car served as a playhouse for Margaret, Lois and Jean, and a private car, fitted out with saloon, observation parlor and kitchen, served for outings with their father. The children thrilled to its whistle, and, occasionally, after they left the smoke-filled city, "Dad" allowed "Martie" to take over the controls.[1] Summers were spent at Lake Wawasee in Indiana, the setting for Margaret's early romantic yearnings.

The qualities which made Arthur Anderson loved by his children were not the qualities needed by his wife, Jessie, in a mate. An insecure woman, raised by an abusive stepmother, Mrs. Anderson felt frustrated in her musical ambitions and, isolated from Indianapolis friends, became a tyrant in the household. Margaret sensed early a "hideous struggle between the sexes," and, looking back, she thought that her parents were both "helpless, absolutely impotent before everything they vaguely felt — two human beings always in the dark, less developed than children."[2] A photograph taken by Mr. Anderson at their last Christmas in Youngstown is a study in family disconnections. "Mother's" eyes avert the camera eye of her husband, and Margaret gazes off into the distance . . . out of the picture toward a world of her own creation.

That world, that something FOR which Margaret lived, would by 1914 be *The Little Review*, an innovative literary magazine she founded and edited in Chicago for the purpose of creating stimulating conversation among writers, artists and anarchists. Of this magazine famed critic Alfred Kazin would write, "Had it not been for the sacrifices and limitless enthusiasm of Margaret Anderson, it is quite likely that [post World War I] American fiction and poetry would have been slower in its experimental course."[3] Fittingly, *The Little Review* had its first home on Michigan Avenue in Chicago's Fine Arts Building, not merely a temple of art, but a work of art in itself.

The summer of 1915 Margaret, with her *Little Review* staff, comprising her sister Lois and recent Vassar graduate Harriet Dean, for want of funds camped out at Highland Park on the shore of Lake Michigan. There she first met Kansan artist Jane

Leyendecker mural in the Fine Arts Building, Chicago home of *The Little Review*, photograph by Mathilda Hills.

Heap, then teaching at Chicago's Lewis Institute. "I know that my real life began with my discovery of Jane's mind — its quality and extensions," Margaret wrote later. "The things I heard her say were unlike the things that other people said — things that 'became known' to her, though she didn't know why or how."[4] Born in 1885 to Norwegian and English parents, Jane and her four siblings grew up on the grounds of the Topeka Asylum for the Insane (now the Menninger Clinic), where her father, George Heap, served as civil engineer. She studied painting and jewelry design at Chicago's Art and Lewis Institutes and as a student fell in love with Florence Reynolds, who would become her lifelong friend and benefactor. After a year abroad with Florence, Jane taught at Lewis, acted with the Chicago Little Theatre and designed sets for Alice Gerstenberg's ground-breaking play *Overtones*.

At the time she met Margaret, Jane had just been rebuffed by a beautiful woman, Alixe Bradley, and decided to "cure herself" by going toward *The Little Review* and Margaret. "If you have a need to receive," Jane said, "I have a need to give."[5] Of a tempestuous nature, daringly original, and gifted with a "cold clear mind that dug at the roots of everything,"[6] Jane challenged Margaret, posing questions she had never even thought to ask. She put "teeth" into Margaret's breathless arguments: " 'Martie,' you should KNOW more."[7] With Jane *The Little Review* took on a new look, each cover more spectacular than its predecessor. The two women formed a familiar sight in

3

Chicago. Margaret at that stage appeared quite frivolous in her dress, ruffles around her throat and cuffs, veils, spectacular hats, while Jane, wearing tailored jackets, stiff shirts, long skirts and an unbecoming pompadour, stomped along beside her.[8]

The two women started working in earnest in Chicago and continued in California and New York, with scarcely a break for nearly seven years, publishing, among others, their favorite poet, Amy Lowell, Sherwood Anderson, Djuna Barnes and anarchist Emma Goldman. At times Jane feared Margaret might be jailed for subversive activities. In New York, mid-1917, they were evicted from their first apartment because Margaret disrupted the conspiracy trial of anti-war activists Emma Goldman and Alexander Berkman.

Settled at last in Greenwich Village, Margaret, in mobcap and dustcoat, edited *The Little Review* as her "housekeeping" venture, while Jane-of-all-trades combined cooking, sewing, painting and carpentry with her editorial duties. Throughout their relationship, Margaret experienced a troubling aspect of Jane — consuming jealousy, initially over *Little Review* staff member Harriet Dean, then Emma Goldman, then their hostess in California, heiress Aline Barnesdale. Margaret felt that she had no freedom: Jane brooded, sulked and even threatened suicide with a revolver kept in a trunk. In 1918 Margaret began an affair with Gladys Tilden, the young niece of Chicago friend Harriet Vaughn Moody. Gladys, who had worshiped the beautiful Margaret from afar in Mrs. Moody's literary salon, was in New York pursuing an acting career. Although Margaret claimed she was not "in love" with Gladys, the affair caused Jane great mental suffering. "How ghastly this is," Margaret wrote Florence Reynolds. "One should be glad of a chance to *do anything* in return for the quite boundless things Jane bestows," but she could not endure Jane's "awful moods . . . crying that is more like moaning."

"What is the matter with me?" she asked Florence Reynolds. "I feel a bondage that I'm impelled to break even if it entails an ultimate loss, the sacrifice of something I wouldn't and shouldn't be without. I can see so perfect a plan of adjusting it all — restoring one's personal freedom (perhaps I should say one's *impersonal* freedom — the very breathing of air that is not poisoned by 'meaning,' 'awareness') — but when we discussed a plan of separate living that seemed to allow of all this and the sharing of interest as well, it developed later that it was one of the things that distressed her. So our plan for next winter is a continuation. . . ."[9]

The following autumn Margaret met the glamorous older woman who was to stir in her romantic yearnings for years to come. The episode began after Gladys visited Sixteenth Street with her new love, Louise Davidson. Margaret listened to tales of Gladys's other aunt, Josephine Plows Day, a former actress rumored to have been the mistress of actor-manager Richard Mansfield. Aunt "Tippy" was in New York from London, arranging to escort young girls on a European tour. Then fifty, "Tippy," dressed in a loose tea gown and heavy silver necklace, had a seventeen-year advantage on Margaret's mastery of charm. Their first meeting is re-envisioned in *Forbidden Fires*:

"She walked slowly toward us. There seemed to be a silence around her, as there would be for a heroine making her first entrance in a stage play. . . . The long silver chain she wore swung to the rhythm of her walk. . . . She seemed so incredibly lovely to me that when she gave me her hand, looking directly into my eyes and saying, 'Ah?', I felt a little movement of pain in my heart."

As an actress in Mansfield's company, "Tippy" had memorized the poetry of Shakespeare and Molière, the prose of Shaw and Ibsen, and had performed in the grand charismatic style. She belonged to a world more subtle than the one to which Margaret had been born — and, like Ibsen's *allumeuse,* Hedda Gabler, she lit fires she had no intention of extinguishing. But the real key to "Tippy's" attractiveness for Margaret lay in her authority. "She could be as dominant as she was seductive" (*Forbidden Fires*).

All fall and winter "Tippy" stayed in New York, giving Margaret something to live for outside drab poverty and the increasingly arduous task of publishing her magazine, by then serializing four lengthy works, among them James Joyce's *Ulysses* and May Sinclair's *Interim*. Just as *The Little Review* entered its final New York phase, bombarded by postal censors, "Tippy" returned to London, vanishing from Margaret's life.

So avant garde had the magazine become with Ezra Pound as its Foreign Editor that it was often confiscated by the U.S. Postal Service and was burned three times for episodes of *Ulysses*. With the appearance of Joyce's "Nausicaa" episode the secretary for the Society for the Prevention of Vice filed a complaint and the editors were arrested, the chief objection being its "too frank description of a woman's dress when the woman was in the clothes described."[10] Asked by a judge "what class of people" the magazine reached, Margaret replied, "The general run of people would as soon read *The Little Review* as take a dose of castor oil."[11] Although ably defended by their lawyer-patron, John Quinn, Margaret and Jane were declared guilty in 1921 of publishing obscene literature, finger-printed, and released on payment of a one-hundred-dollar fine. Not one New York newspaper supported these courageous women, nor would Joyce's *Ulysses* pass censorship in the United States until 1933. Margaret, like the heroine of *Forbidden Fires,* had always "pursued her life as if no one dared to criticize her about anything." She began to weary of the fight. After seven years of struggle, introducing readers to Modernism, Margaret expressed anger at the literary establishment. Of a talk given by novelist Ford Madox Ford she wrote: "velleities of what we used to talk when we first started the L.R. — and he is applauded as a 'modern' and listened to with interest, because he is a man. . . . One gets madder every day!"[12]

Margaret was turning away from literature — and from Jane — to her first passion, music, when, a few weeks after the *Ulysses* verdict, through pianist friend Allen Tanner she met and fell deeply in love with French actress-singer Georgette Leblanc, ex-common-law wife of Nobel prizewinning playwright Maurice Maeterlinck. What struck Margaret most were Georgette's unsurpassable smile and charm and a look she especially loved, "just a bit worn (though not really at all), a suggestion that she has had rich experience."[13] Acclaimed for singing Thais and Carmen and for acting in Maeterlinck's plays, she had antici-pated singing the lead in an operatic version of his *Pelléas et*

Mélisande, but composer Debussy objected, giving the role instead to youthful Mary Garden — Margaret's diva in Chicago days. Critics today agree that Georgette Leblanc inspired a new phase in Maeterlinck's career, serving as the model for his empowered heroines and women of majesty, replacing the pale creatures of his Symbolist plays.[14] Tension built between the two, however, when she discovered herself quoted in Maeterlinck's books as "an old philosopher" and "an old friend." On being questioned, he replied:

"I steal from you, don't I? But, don't you see, it would be ridiculous to mention you. You're on the stage, a singer. Nobody would believe me!"[15]

By the time Georgette reached America after World War I, not speaking a word of English, she had lost both husband and career but had written two books under her own name, including *The Children's Bluebird,* and hoped to publish her memoirs in the Hearst newspapers. At first Margaret volunteered to edit an English version of Georgette's manuscript. Later, often concealed behind a painted backdrop, she accompanied Georgette on the piano during recitals of songs by Poulenc, Milhaud, and de Falla. With this older woman Margaret found "what real love is like — a bond of mutual understanding"[16] — in an atmosphere without the tension which existed in ordinary

Georgette Leblanc in
The Bluebird
ca. 1911.

human relationships. Their love, spanning twenty years, is celebrated in *The Fiery Fountains,* the second volume of Margaret's romanticized autobiography:

"We cannot have met by chance, Georgette and I, since we knew at once that we were to join hands and advance through life together. Ah, I said, when I first saw her marvelous mystic face: this is the land I have been seeking; I left home long ago to discover it — a new continent, an unearthly place, the great world of art. . . . For twenty years I listened to her words, always with the feeling that I was being blessed or rescued."

Margaret's gift to Georgette was a renewed sense of life: "But I alone know what Margaret has given in private," Georgette wrote in her memoir *La Machine à Courage.*[17]

During performances at their intimate cellar "Theatre Club" at 47 Washington Square South, a wealthy sewing-machine manufacturer offered to endow Georgette on a European concert tour. She was given an office overlooking the Hudson River and Central Park, and Gladys's companion, Louise Davidson, became her manager. In late May 1923, Georgette and her *dame de compagnie,* former Belgian schoolteacher Monique Serrure, and Margaret set sail for France. Aboard the S.S. *Paris* Margaret described her ecstasy in a letter to Allen Tanner, then in

Margaret, departing for France, 1923.

8

Berlin — and her difficult parting from Jane:

"Dear, dear, dear Narcisse!!!
    Couldn't write a line all these months: had much too much to say — and now as I regard the sea from this charming little writing room of the "Paris," I can only tell you that everything is much more éclatant, interesting and amusing than you can possibly imagine and that you'll be fully repaid by waiting a few days more for our conversation.... Georgette's "Art Direction Georgette Leblanc, Inc." ... is really a little too astounding but really true. Also she is in way of becoming a millionaire with a group of real gagas who thrust money at her and include me. The story of all this is dramatic and sentimental beyond words, and I demand one night — you and she and I and Monique alone — to do it justice. As for me, I spent the last three weeks in N.Y. in a charming room in the Brevoort from which issued every day famous "scraps of paper" to all my friends who are now very violent enemies — masterpieces. They had got so desperate with me that they began to attack me by the post since I refused them my presence. All the celebrated documents have been preserved for your delectation. I began to have the feeling of a very charming *fauve*.... Nothing so invigorating in the world.
    Well — we shall talk. I adore you as always! Can't wait to see you and it seems to me you must come to Paris first to find us — so many things arranged. But

The Château de Tancarville on the Seine estuary.

we'll wire you instantly. I am quite mad — be prepared. . . .[18]

From Le Havre the three women were driven toward Paris, and along the Seine estuary Margaret saw rising from high rocks a fabulous fairy castle — the medieval Château de Tancarville. "Yes," said Georgette, hearing her exclamations, "that's where my sister lives."

"But why didn't you tell me you had a sister in a castle?"

"Château life has never interested me," was Georgette's only reply.[19]

One week later Jane arrived in Paris, insisting on meetings with the now-famous expatriate writers and artists published in *The Little Review,* Joyce, Gertrude Stein, Ezra Pound, Tristan Tzara and Constantin Brancusi. That same summer, when Lois Anderson fell desperately ill, Jane proceeded to co-adopt, with Margaret, Lois's two sons, Tom and Fritz Peters, thus forging a legal bond with her lost love.

By August Georgette's millionaire backer withdrew, hearing rumors spread by Jane of Georgette's lesbian liaison. The glorious tour came to an end. Her singing career at a standstill, Georgette accepted the leading role in a silent film directed by Marcel L'Herbier, *L'Inhumaine,* playing the aging diva Claire Lescot, a predecessor to Norma Desmond, the self-obsessed movie queen of *Sunset Boulevard.* The women then returned to America for a coast-to-coast concert tour, which was an artistic success and a financial disaster.

Urged by Jane, they attended lectures in New York by Georges I. Gurdjieff, a Russian philosopher, part mystic, part P. T. Barnum, director of the Institute for the Harmonious Development of Man at Fontainebleau, near Paris.[20] Gurdjieff taught that human beings merely sleepwalk unless awakened to consciousness through stages of shocks and self-observation: "Man has no soul; he has only the potentiality."[21] Margaret's interest in Gurdjieff reflected her ongoing concern with psychology since early *Little Review* days. In 1924 she gave over her magazine to Jane and, with Georgette and Monique, left for France and the Institute at Fontainebleau. That summer Margaret began seriously to write. One of Gurdjieff's exercises called for isolation for at least an hour of quietness, not permitting the mind to wander, but concentrating on "aim of life."[22] "You realize what crimes you've done," she wrote, "letting your life be all cut up by a million ridiculous struggles . . . using your life blood to keep *The Little Review* going. How I could have lived that way for so long — Well, God knows, it made me nervous enough." Out of this exercise came the idea for writing her own life: "I think I'll call it 'The 30 Years War — the Autobiography of a Resisting Nature.' "[23]

In Paris Georgette launched colossal schemes for performances, first in the Bois de Boulogne, then on a rotting Seine barge, and the last by a portal of Notre Dame Cathedral. All of them failed, and she had to face the truth: Maeterlinck's plays were outmoded and her early stage successes ignored. Reduced to giving recitals of poetry and song, she toured Italy, Belgium and Spain, performed at the Salle Pleyel in Paris. The Prince von Thurn und Taxis invited Georgette to his castle at Duino on the Adriatic Sea, and there, to Margaret's piano accompaniment, she acted the boy-saint in D'Annunzio's *Le Martyre de Saint Sebastien.*

So praised was Margaret by a Paris reviewer for her polished technique, her spirited playing and her beauty that she still hoped for a piano career.[24] During a winter when all concerts were canceled and Georgette recuperated from an illness in Cannes "with some rich idiot," Margaret, alone in their Left Bank apartment, practiced the piano day in and day out. Without any money of her own, she dressed in French workmen's jeans and was so ashamed of her looks that for two weeks she never went outdoors. Approaching forty, Margaret's outlook was changing. Drab poverty had become a way of life. She began to feel an intense longing for the glamorous "Tippy," and in early spring she wrote to Gladys Tilden, asking for photographs and letters Gladys had kept.

But hadn't Gurdjieff warned Margaret that she lived in a romantic day-dreaming sort of love? He had asked her bluntly, "What's the matter with you — are you afraid to have a physical affair?"[25] Within a few months she met freedom-loving, work-loving Solita Solano Wilkinson, American writer familiar to

Left Bank residents as companion to Janet Flanner of the *New Yorker*'s "Paris Letter." Solita was a vibrant personality with large "swimming eyes of intense blue"[26] and dark hair cut short. No one since Jane so criticized, challenged and stimulated Margaret. Restless as she was, Margaret gave in to Solita's great magnetism, and Solita fell wildly in love. Forever after Solita would mark on her calendar February 19th, the day when they met in 1927. The life story Margaret told her new love became, with Solita's expert editing, the published version of *My Thirty Years' War*.

Solita was demonstrative, but Margaret, who never spontaneously embraced her friends, was shameless in love, passionately embracing Solita in a taxi, as if the driver did not exist. Remembering Margaret, friends said that she was even more beautiful then than photographs show. Her lovely voice was different from anyone's, lightly husky, with a softness to the edges of her words, and her laugh was like tinkling bells. She had great physical allure, waved a perfumed chiffon handkerchief under her nostrils, wore a ruffled white blouse, beads and antique silver bracelets à la Nancy Cunard, but beneath this allure one could feel a fire that was spiritual.[27]

Naturally Solita took Margaret at once to Chartres, whose unique spire was the central symbol of her most recent novel, *This Way Up*: "The Cathedral was built not for God, but for a woman."[28] Only on weekends were they together, but Solita by now had her own room at the Hotel St. Germain, and, at Margaret's urging they locked themselves up, ordered meals sent in, danced endlessly to the gramophone, made love. Solita stopped writing fiction; poems spilled out instead, such as "Profile," expressing the intensity of her emotion — and her dread of losing Margaret:

> As we sit head near head in this bed
> Our books beside the dinner tray
> I think while you refuse another pear
> Of the unlived years through which I lived
> When you were not yet there. . . .

Margaret Anderson.
Photograph by Victor
Georg, New York,
ca. 1921.

But now I watch your profiled head
Against the pillows of this bed
Your head that turns as does no other
As you light a cigarette and lightly ask the hour
I'm dragging at the minute hand. . . .

I take away the tray and turn
To see you turn a page
How angel white the light
Where your profile burns the curtain
And the arc of arm, how certain
As you turn and read of death
As a theory to discern
But I know you'll go away one day
Oh where are you?
And I live death through
Here before you.[29]

Georgette regarded the affair as an infatuation until she met
Solita and recognized her power, but Georgette was practiced in
the art of life. Having lost Maeterlinck through her possessive-
ness, she did not repeat her error. She understood well
Margaret's need for personal freedom, the sole gift that could

bind Margaret to another human being. Jane, however, newly returned to Paris after her Machine Age Exposition in New York, regarded Solita as a threat to her collaboration with Margaret on a final number of *The Little Review,* and the two became instant enemies.

Christmas found Margaret so broke that when she went to the Galeries Lafayette to buy presents, she left without paying and was arrested. Her release came quickly because Solita arranged a lineup of character witnesses: two rows of lesbians in dark suits, each with a gardenia in her buttonhole. To the generosity of Solita, by then a Paris correspondent for a Detroit magazine, the *D.A.C. News,* Margaret owed her particular chic, with fashionable clothes bought from English couturier Elspeth Champcommunal, Jane's new love. And thus Georgette, dependent on her brother, detective writer Maurice Leblanc, for support, was relieved of financial responsibility for Margaret, who admitted, "The one thing I could NOT stand would be to have to occupy myself with the money problem."[30] The French might say of this otherwise liberated woman, *Elle est entretenue* — she is a kept woman. Gurdjieff warned her of "parasitism." From Margaret's perspective, however, an exchange took place. She accepted money and *les cadeaux,* but she always gave generously of herself in return, and for a time she paid highly for what she received with a loss of liberty. Letters detailing Margaret's current finances seem at odds with her romantic "life on a cloud" but actually underscore her dual nature: "fifty/fifty Imagination and Reality,"[31] the very qualities which enabled her to found *The Little Review.*

The Château de la Muette in the Forest of St. Germain-en-Laye.

In 1931 Margaret felt secure in the love of Georgette and in her love affair with Solita. With money from her just-published memoirs, the improvident Georgette leased La Muette, an impossibly romantic, broken-down Louis XIV château just west of Paris in the Forest of St. Germain-en-Laye. La Muette fostered an escape mentality in Margaret. She read Stendhal's treatise *De L'Amour* and Constant's novel *Adolphe,* identifying with the emotions of the hero, never the heroine. Deep in the forest of chestnut trees life was lived in a perpetual trance. Georgette "staged" a musical soirée; their guests were composer Darius Milhaud, playwright Luigi Pirandello, film director Germaine Dulac, Gladys and Louise, and Solita. Elspeth Champcommunal arrived without Jane, newly hospitalized with diabetes. Joyce was absent also, lost with his wife, Nora, and son *en route* through the Forest of St. Germain. The château façade and great Rotonde provided a stage set for Georgette, dressed in a clinging scarlet gown and matching turban above her crown of blond hair, as she sang the role of Mélisande; "backstage," however, were peeling wallpaper and waterless faucets.[32]

Margaret's passionate love affair with Solita had begun to cool when she renewed a correspondence with "Tippy." "Tippy's" letters reek of the Edwardian stage:

"I feel that I should write to you in golden ink. . . . There has not been a moment of forgetfulness. I am radiant of heart, as if an elixir had been introduced into my food and sleep."[33]

Solita, to her later regret, discovered a letter from "Tippy" and in a fury of jealousy informed her that Margaret was known to be lesbian — this only a few years after Radclyffe Hall's *Well of Loneliness* was judged obscene in a notorious London court case. An ardent follower of Frank Buchman's Oxford Group, forerunner of "Moral Re-Armament," "Tippy" responded predictably, drawing on the full arsenal of the New Testament to instruct Solita, "On this Crucifixion Day, I want you to know that I long for you to be redeemed and made clear . . . die to your sin."[34] When Margaret learned the truth, she charged Solita with base treachery — the worst thing a friend can do to a friend. In

15

all probability she struck Solita. Soon Margaret received a "renouncement" from "Tippy." Convinced that lesbianism was a vice so soul-destroying to the character that unless one can combat it, one should in no wise countenance it, "Tippy" decided that they must not meet again. And so ashamed was Solita that, although she became Margaret's most loyal friend, she was never again completely at ease in her presence.[35]

Meanwhile the world was rapidly changing. Panic selling hit the dollar in France, and Georgette had to give up the Château de La Muette. By winter it was "just a tragic struggle to find money or some immediate way of keeping alive,"[36] and Georgette with her little family moved to her sister's Napoleonic house in the Paris suburb of Le Pecq. In 1933, when they were able to arrange a getaway, they left for the Bavarian Alps with Jane, her old friend Florence Reynolds, Solita, Janet Flanner and Janet's new love, Noel Haskins Murphy. *En route* they stopped at a cheap guest house filled with Nazis, singing their anthem. Next day, according to Solita's account in the *D.A.C. News,* a huge man in leather shorts rushed at them and shook his fist, and an officer in Nazi uniform announced, "You may not wear trousers."

"Why not?"

"German women must all wear skirts."

"But we are not German women. We are Americans."

"You must dress like German women. You will proceed to your car at once and leave the town."[37]

Margaret could bear no more. She rushed Georgette and Solita back to France where, she said, lesbians were treated like "a charming race."

In an attempt to rekindle love, Margaret sent "Tippy" a tiny carved crèche from Oberammergau. To this overture "Tippy" responded with an invitation to travel. On journeys to Vienna and Budapest they played an ongoing "cat-and-mouse" game — with Margaret the "mouse" — until Margaret broke away from the woman with whom she was "violently in love."[38]

And Solita, in despair over loss of love, sought out Gurdjieff, to whose teachings Margaret had introduced her. His institute now abandoned, he formed a small study group in early 1936, exclusively women, with Solita, Louise Davidson, Kathryn Hulme

16

(later to write *The Nun's Story*) and her love, self-made millionaire hat designer Alice Rohrer. Jane visited occasionally, having moved to London with Elspeth, then chief designer for Worth. That June, at Solita's urging, Margaret and Georgette joined the Gurdjieff group. Inspired anew by reports of his teaching, Margaret formulated a "position" paper on her own sexual nature, disclosing the powerful influence on her generation of lesbians of Richard von Krafft-Ebing's *Psychopathia Sexualis* as well as her own ways of coping with difference. She mailed these pages, unedited, to Jane with the admonition, "I am trying to keep everyone's hands off, especially my own."

As I grew up I never felt that my position in love involved any sexual confusion. I realized that I was in the minority but I was already accustomed to the idea of the important minority in all major concerns of life — I had always known that the majority was wrong. My situation seemed to me unique. There was nothing masculine about me from bracelets to ruffles. I suppose "*androgyne*" covers the conditionment I am describing. I can feel like a child, a girl, a boy, or a man, but I cannot feel like a woman. I haven't the remotest connection with this alien race. The need I understand is to bestow passion and to receive tenderness.
I have never spoken these words to any human being, for one reason because it is inconceivable to me that anyone could love me as much as I love "them."[39]

Threatened by the loss of her illusions, Margaret felt extremely uncomfortable in Gurdjieff's presence. Periodically, over two and a half years, he created situations designed to make her acknowledge the falsehood of her romantic flower-in-the-buttonhole pose. Perhaps then, and only then, he said, might she have something of her own. Mostly he met with resistance. "It was all right to have sex," Margaret recalled, "but all wrong (psychopathic) to be 'in love.' Well you can see now how difficult everything was for me *chez* Gurdjieff; everything that he wanted for me was against my nature, against all that I had ever felt or been."[40] He shocked her with allusions to bodily

17

functions she never in her life mentioned and with gross references to lesbian lovemaking.[41] Only the promise of replacing emptiness with the power to make conscious choices drew her back to his table each time.

Two emblems capture the spirit of Margaret Anderson during the decade of the thirties. First, Berenice Abbott's Paris portrait,

Margaret Anderson, photograph by Berenice Abbott, Paris, 1930.

taken in 1930 for the frontispiece of *My Thirty Years' War*, shows a glamorous woman in toque and gloves, accustomed to her beauty, gazing at the camera with limitless self-assurance. This is the legendary *Little Review* publisher of James Joyce, Gertrude Stein and Ernest Hemingway. The closing sentences of her autobiography form a motto characterizing her at this stage:

I am trying to become a new human being. I still make vows to achieve an increasingly beautiful life.

Paris, 1929

Then, paired with this emblem, place another, its motto an outcry to Jane from the south of France a decade later when Georgette Leblanc lay dying,

I begin not to know what to do[42]

accompanied by a snapshot of Margaret at the railroad station in Cannes during the war as she said goodbye to her world. Her head is tilted charmingly as in the Berenice Abbott portrait, but now she appears worn, visibly aged, and vulnerable — truly "a new human being." The 1930s represent a time of folly and reflection for Margaret — the folly relating to her mid-life infatuation, and the reflection to an inner struggle with the

Margaret at the railway station in Cannes, 1942.

teaching of Gurdjieff, culminating, in tragedy, with a different sense of who she is.

From the glorious countryside of Normandy in September 1938 Margaret wrote, "I must feel the autumn come on." Then came the first war scare, and Georgette persuaded her with Monique to cross to England on the channel ferry. In London, Margaret saw "Tippy" and acknowledged at last, "I know that 'Tippy' does not care at all about me." That "war" proved to be a phony one, but by spring 1939 the real war began, and not long after Hitler's invasions of Czechoslovakia, Margaret's private world fell to pieces: a doctor diagnosed a lump in Georgette's breast as cancerous. After rushing back and forth between Gurdjieff and a quack London "doctor" named Ruth Drown, they took Gladys's suggestion to consult a specialist near where she lived in Cannes. His verdict: "Cancer. Operate immediately. Probably remove the breast." Margaret made up a story to tell Georgette that a benign tumor could become dangerous. Next morning she wrote to Jane, "Oh — what hell here last night after the consultation, but at least she's up again today."[43]

Hitler was invading Poland as they returned to Paris, and amidst rumors of bombings, Georgette entered a makeshift hospital. Margaret refused to leave France despite orders from the American embassy, and early one morning, at a fogbound crossroads west of Paris, she bade farewell to Solita and Janet on their way to Bordeaux. As soon as she could leave the clinic, Georgette was taken to Solita's old room at the Hotel St. Germain. Next door Margaret escaped into mystery novels in "the drugged pursuit of crime" — until she remembered Gurdjieff's words: "Man must always prepare for what he does, necessary at all time that he THINKS what he does, only THIS is life."[44] And prepare she did, driving Georgette, Monique and a few belongings from Paris to Biarritz, and from Biarritz to the Riviera and back again, crisscrossing France, with each move just escaping the war, until finally she settled Georgette, Monique and herself at Le Cannet in the Chalet Rose on the Avenue Victoria, a tiny cottage perched among eucalyptus and almond trees above the "heartbreakingly blue" Mediterranean. There, imprisoned in a war, knowing Georgette was doomed, they lived until her death.

The woman who wrote in 1929 "I am trying to become a new human being" did not foresee that she must one day give up "an increasingly beautiful life," but that was "many years ago, when [she] was living happily ever after." In 1941, with a shortage of morphine to curb Georgette's agonizing pain, life became real, as Margaret wrote Jane, "—I mean a real hell: constant unflagging illness. I begin not to know what to do."[45]

Gurdjieff, by confronting Margaret with the falsehood in her life and by giving her lessons in life's "undependability," helped prepare her to face her greatest enemy, reality. She endured the destruction of her private world to become — as in the 1942 snapshot of Margaret with a flower in her buttonhole, boarding the train at Cannes for the hazardous passage to America — a woman worn, but with "a suggestion that she has had rich experience."

As an exhausted Margaret sailed out of Lisbon aboard the S.S. *Drottningholm*, crowded with refugees, she tried to forget where she was and where she was going, seeing only the grave she was leaving behind. The second day at sea, she began to make a "Gurdjieff effort," and it allowed her "in the most effortless way to LIVE what he had taught" her.[46] Sitting on the promenade deck, she watched a tall blond woman in blue, "that summer blue of Cannes, always worn with a touch of red,"[47] leave her chair and walk across the deck. Margaret learned that Dorothy Caruso, widow of the great singer, Enrico Caruso, had been stranded in France with her two daughters and, at the outbreak of war as the guest of expatriate Isabelle Pell, had worked for the Resistance in Auribeau. As if the reward of her Gurdjieff effort had to come quickly, Margaret fell into a new love central to her life for years to come.

At the pier in Jersey City where the *Drottningholm* docked on the fourth of July, Solita, Kathryn Hulme, Alice Rohrer and Janet Flanner cheered, prepared to offer Margaret whatever help she might need. No one felt a greater responsibility than Solita, who had written offering Margaret her apartment, neglecting to mention that she had fallen in love and was living with a stunning young woman she had met and courted in the American Women's Voluntary Service, Elizabeth Jenks Clark. When Margaret walked down the gangplank with an artificial carnation in her buttonhole, looking pale and thin, no one was more surprised — and relieved — to see her arm-in-arm with another woman than was Solita: "I understood, so many things when you arrived that I was paralyzed. I understood that you hadn't arrived at all, that you weren't going to arrive." And Janet Flanner, who had found in Italian-born Natalia Murray her ideal companion, quipped, "There have never been so many happy endings since Gilbert and Sullivan!"[48]

For thirteen years Dorothy and Margaret shared their lives in America, with frequent visits after the war to Paris and Le Cannet, where Monique remained. Dorothy wrote two books of memoirs with Margaret's encouragement, one of which formed the background for the Mario Lanza film *The Great Caruso,* and Margaret, with the help of Solita's "scathing editing," completed *The Fiery Fountains.* This transcendental account of love, with its "furious idealism concentrated wholly on personal relationships," reminded Alfred Kazin of the great "romantic tragedies in Fitzgerald and Hemingway." [49]

In November 1952 Dorothy underwent a radical mastectomy in Baltimore, and Margaret wrote her sister Lois: "I'm a nurse eighteen hours a day. Her wound is frightful — a real mutilation, not at all a simple line cut like Georgette's."[50] For three years Dorothy struggled bravely, not only to survive cancer, but to share a normal life with Margaret and with her family, one summer renting a villa in Cannes so Margaret could be near Monique in the Chalet Rose. Occasionally they visited Solita and Elizabeth in Morristown, New Jersey, and it was to them Margaret turned in need when Dorothy died.

"She had such plans for our future. I had such plans for her. Her death was so unbearably human, and my desolation seems too deep to cure. Today it snowed and I rushed out to buy seed for her birds. . . . I AM all right, but I hear myself walking through the house crying out loud like an animal. . . . Now I know what loneliness is."[51]

With a generous annuity from Dorothy, Margaret was free to make decisions about her own life, and when Solita and

Elizabeth planned a permanent move to France, to a little house in Orgeval rented from Noel Murphy, Margaret had no difficulty making up her mind. "I'll sail for France in April, with you, and stay there for the rest of my life!"[52]

As she settled into a simple life once again with Monique in the Chalet Rose — a primitive cottage by today's standards — Margaret began to create and sustain an atmosphere which was the result of the way she lived her entire life. She couldn't stop suffering over Dorothy's death. Then one night she thought, "What could I concentrate on that would take my memories off Duffy?"[53] At two A.M. she wakened with the whole conception of a novel in her mind, went straight to the typewriter and tapped out the preface, the first scene and the last scene. She worked through her continuing grief to regain a sense of the continuity of life in the only way she knew — by writing and reliving her own romantic past.

For Lois, Margaret described her feelings at the time: "I'm working so madly, at least eight hours a day, on my new short book. . . . No time for anything except a long promenade every day. I walk the three km. down to Cannes easily, but almost never go because of book. Have to keep concentrated and on a schedule or I'll never accomplish it. . . . On December 16 it will be a year since D. died. Only the book I'm doing keeps my thoughts off this incredible fact."[54]

The novel fictionalizes an episode contemporary with and totally absent from Margaret Anderson's autobiography *The Fiery Fountains,* but woven into it are the two women most important to her — Georgette Leblanc as the châtelaine, "Claire Lescaut," and Jane Heap as the stalwart London friend, "Kaye." Elspeth Champcommunal figures briefly as "Eleanor." And always in the background lies the lost world of the Château de la Muette outside of Paris, where Margaret experienced her most intense romantic yearnings for "Tippy" — the seductive *allumeuse* "Audrey Leigh" of *Forbidden Fires.*

Tap, tap, tap, tap. TAP, tap, tap, TAP, tap. . . .
Through destruction and bereavement Margaret entered a

new cycle o. ᴜᴦe — one which left her, "at the end of things, with a new beginning."[55] She would write two more books, *The Unknowable Gurdjieff*, dedicated to Jane Heap, and *The Strange Necessity*, the final volume of her autobiography, composed at the Hotel Reine des Prés in the village of Le Cannet after the death of Monique and dedicated to Solita Solano "with my love, admiration and gratitude." Margaret Anderson died of emphysema on October 19, 1973, and is buried beside Georgette Leblanc and Mathilde Serrure (Monique) in the Cimitère des Anges, Le Cannet.

NOTES

Abbreviations:
BC Henry W. and Albert A. Berg Collection, New York Public Library, Astor, Lenox and Tilden Foundations.
FER The Florence E. Reynolds Collection related to Jane Heap and *The Little Review*, University of Delaware Library, Newark, Delaware.
EJC Elizabeth Jenks Clark.
F-S Flanner-Solano Collection, Library of Congress, Washington, D.C.
HRC Harry Ransom Humanities Research Center, University of Texas at Austin.
JH Jane Heap.
LA Lois Anderson (Karinsky).
MCA Margaret C. Anderson. Unless otherwise identifed, quotations from her unpublished letters and papers and those of Solita Solano are in private collections.
SS Solita Solano.

1. Personal interviews with the late Lois Anderson Karinsky, 7–12 May 1978.
2. MCA, Letter to LA, 1 May, 1930, BC.
3. *The New York Times Book Review*, 16 August 1970, p. 1.
4. MCA papers. Jane Heap is recognized today for her genius, and Yale University Professor of Computer Science David Gelernter credits her 1927 international Exposition linking art and the machine as "a milestone."
5. MCA Letters to EJC, 4 April 1971; 25 October, 1964.

6. Fanny Butcher, review of *My Thirty Years' War*, in *Chicago Tribune*, n.d. (ca. 30 May 1930).
7. JH quoted in MCA notes.
8. According to Bernadine Szold, letter to Dale Kramer, 30 Nov. 1963, The Newberry Library, Chicago.
9. MCA letter to Florence E. Reynolds, 8 August 1918, FER.
10. *The New York Times*, 22 February 1921, p. 6.
11. Quoted in John Quinn, letter to Judge W. H. Lamar, 19 June 1919, Manuscript Collection, New York Public Library.
12. "The Reader Critic," *The Little Review*, Vol. 10, No. 2 (Winter 1924–25), 60.
13. Letter to Allen Tanner, n.d., February 1965, HRC.
14. Bettina Knapp, *Maurice Maeterlinck*, p. 92. .
15. Quoted in Georgette Leblanc, *Souvenirs: My Life with Maeterlinck*, pp. 135–9.
16. MCA notes.
17. *The Fiery Fountains* (1st ed.), pp. 6–7; Georgette Leblanc, *La Machine à Courage: Souvenirs, p. 82: "mais je suis seule à savoir tout ce qu'elle m'a donné en secret."*
18. Letter to Allen Tanner, n.d., HRC.
19. *My Thirty Years' War*, 2nd ed., p. 242.
20. Gurdjieff, the son of a Greek father and Armenian mother, is said to have been born in Kars (Alexandropol) in either 1872 or 1877. See James Webb, *The Harmonious Circle*.
21. Margaret C. Anderson, *The Unknowable Gurdjieff* (reprint, 1973), p. 25.
22. Georges I. Gurdjieff, *Meetings with Remarkable Men* (reprint, 1969), p. 301.
23. Letter to LA, n.d., ca. August 1924, BC.
24. Newspaper clipping encl. in letter to LA, 11 Nov. 1939, BC.
25. G. I. Gurdjieff, MCA notebook.
26. SS and Janet Flanner, unpublished notes, F-S.
27. Personal interviews with Angèle B. Levesque, 9 May 1983; 8 January 1978.
28. SS, *This Way Up*, p. 161.
29. "Profile," in *Statue in a Field*.
30. Letter to LA, n.d., Dec. 1928, BC.
31. MCA, Letter to Allen Tanner, n.d., HRC.
32. Kathryn Hulme, *The Undiscovered Country*, pp. 55–6.
33. Notebook, MCA papers.
34. Letter to SS, 3 March 1932.
35. EJC.

36. MCA, letter to LA, 23 January 1933, BC.
37. SS, "Both Banks of the Seine" in *D.A.C. News* (October 1933), pp. 33–5, F-S.
38. Letter to Gladys Plows Tilden, 26 October 1966.
39. Richard von Krafft-Ebing, *Psychopathia Sexualis*. The April 1916 *Little Review*, Vol. 3, No. 2, advertises this translation "sold only to physicians, jurists, clergymen and educators." The phrase "I felt like a man" frequently appears in Krafft-Ebing's case histories. Letter to JH, n.d., ca. April 1936.
40. Letter to Kathryn Hulme, 2 July 1958, Yale Collection of American Literature, Beinecke Rare Book and Manuscript Library, Yale University.
41. SS, "Unedited Notes," ca. February 1937.
42. *My Thirty Years' War* (2nd ed.), p. 274; letter to JH, 25 March 1940.
43. Letters to JH, n.d., ca. September 1938 and ca. September 1939.
44. MCA, *The Fiery Fountains* (2nd ed.), p. 176; MCA Notes.
45. Letter to JH, 25 March 1940.
46. Letter to Florence E. Reynolds, 7 August 1942, FER.
47. MCA, *The Strange Necessity*, p. 180.
48. SS letter to MCA, n.d.; MCA quoted Janet Flanner in a letter to Florence E. Reynolds, 3 October 1942, FER.
49. Alfred Kazin, *The New York Times Book Review*, 16 August 1970, p. 1.
50. Letter to LA, 1 January 1953, BC.
51. Letter to EJC, 30 January 1956; letter to Janet Flanner, 1 January 1956, F-S.
52. Letter to EJC, February 1956.
53. Letter to LA, 23 September 1958, BC.
54. Letter to LA, 27 October 1956, BC.
55. MCA, *The Strange Necessity*, p. 198.

FORBIDDEN FIRES

"Charme de l'amour, qui pourrait . . . vous décrire!"
("Oh, magic of love, who could . . . describe you!"

—Benjamin Constant, *Adolphe*

The Beginning

— 1 —

The story I want to tell, and which I love to remember, began on an old-fashioned summer day. . . .

As usual, we had gone to the lake in June, and all summer our lake-side cottage was filled with music — piano music and the murmur of water. These were the elements in which I floated through the long and lovely hours.

We had an old mahogany square piano, too ancient and beautiful for beautiful sound, but which served our needs for the two days after arrival until a good piano could be sent in from the village. From then until the end of September anyone passing along the lake-front could stop and listen to a concert of Chopin's most haunting music.

The cottage stood a few yards from the lake, with a shaded path between it and the water that slapped softly against the pier. A canoe, a steel rowboat with "feather" oars, a motor launch and a small sailboat rocked slowly on the lake. To the right of the pier there was a leaning oak tree whose branches hung out over the water. Around it a low stone wall had been built on which you could sit, under the tree's heavy branches, and plan what you wanted from life.

What I wanted was love; and it was what I found.

I was eighteen, it was June, I was entranced by the cadence of music and flowing water, and it was in this melodious place that my great experience of romantic love had its beginning.

Later I was to know real love — boundless, changeless, deathless. But the romantic miracle lasted for thirty years, like a prolonged adolescence; and though it had an ending, it never came to an end.

* * * * *

31

Day by day, all the boys who were supposed to stir our young hearts strolled along the path between cottages and lake. I can still remember their names, I can still count ten of them who, I was told, were in love with me. One day a girl who lived in the cottage next door confided to me, "Every night I wish on a star to be as popular as you are." These words were pleasing, but meant little to me. I thought the girl was prettier than I was, and, since she was so interested in boys, wondered why they didn't choose her instead of me? *I* was interested in pianos.

Our cottage porch was furnished like a living-room, with a deep red carpet and white lounge-chairs cushioned in green. There was a low wide swing piled with green pillows, and a round table which held vases of white flowers. Beside them stood a large crystal bowl, always filled with slices of fresh pineapple.

One night a boy sat beside me on the swing, trying to speak of love. I heard him say in a strangled voice, "I know I'm being too persistent in the face of your indifference." This didn't seem to me an inspired approach, but then whom did I know who was inspired? Myself, I answered; and this was true — I really thought that I was a repository of unparalleled, unrecognized or untalked-of emotions, acquainted with an effulgence that no one else shared or demanded. I listened to people's talk about ideas, or about love, and discovered that none of it offered any challenge to my own standards or feelings. The boy's fumbling words made me uncomfortable, and I made an effort to find a kind way of asking him, "Then why persist?" But at that moment the girl next door began to play a Chopin nocturne and all I said to the boy was, "Listen! How wonderful!"

He listened for a few minutes, then said goodnight and strode away — defiant and ineffectual. I watched him go, unmoved. How could I listen to his halting emotions while Chopin was so lyrically expressing my own? The nocturne floated out over the lake, like a shining light on the water, and I listened with all my being, convinced that such magic was all I asked of life. When at last the music ended I left the porch in a daze and went up to my flower-filled bedroom.

I had chosen a room at the back of the cottage instead of on the lake-front because its windows looked over acres of wheatfields, and at midnight a distant train sent its whistle through the wheat — a long sound, a rest for the heart. Night after mysterious night I listened for this sound, and once when I was very ill I lay in this room listening to Chopin all day. Our music teacher had been invited to the lake to play for me, since that was all I asked for. Between breakfast and lunch she played waltzes and mazurkas, and my favorite Fantasy-Impromptu. Between lunch and tea she played all the études, and between tea and dinner the twenty-four preludes. Still I hadn't had enough; so after dinner she played nocturnes. Her love of Chopin was as enduring as mine, and the day seemed to have been as happy for her as it was life-giving to me.

. . . The train whistle ran through the night, toward far cities where I would one day go, alone and free, and live only for music, love, poetry and magnificent ideas.

And then, one day . . . my great experience began.

. . . A golden summer afternoon, and friends of mother's were coming to tea, bringing with them a guest from London. I usually avoided teas, but the word "London" held a spell for me; so I waited with the others for the guest to appear.

She walked slowly toward us, under the summer trees, holding out her hand to mother. She was so different from anyone I had ever seen that I thought she must be a great actress. There was a kind of silence around her, as there would be for a heroine making her first entrance in a stage play. Her friends served merely as a background; she stood out from them like a legendary figure moving within the boundary of her own irradiation. The long silver chain she wore swung to the rhythm of her walk with a sound of soft chimes. She seemed so incredibly lovely to me that when she gave me her hand, looking directly into my eyes and saying "Ah?," I felt a little movement of pain in my heart.

Afterward I sat in a far corner of the porch, barely conscious of voices and the tinkle of tea-cups. From time to time she looked at me and smiled slowly, and I thought I had never seen so beautiful a face — more than beautiful, some power in it I had never felt before, stillness and swift changes, something so compelling that I couldn't fix her features on my mind or even remember them later. But I remembered ever afterward a mirage that appeared as the afternoon light began to fade — a changed *mise en scène* as if a camera had photographed a different assemblage: the porch suddenly became as dark as night, the people and objects on it disappeared and only she remained, sitting in a circle of light which held in its center a large topaz ring and the whiteness of her dramatic hands.

The day was fading, as if a storm were coming, and everyone began to talk of leaving before the rain fell. But mother, charmed by the new guest, urged her to stay to dinner. "Thank you," I heard the blurred voice say, "I think I should love to." And she smiled at me again.

By dinner time the storm had become violent and we were all nervous. From our living-room windows high waves rushed toward us as if they would enter the cottage. The brilliance of the lightning made us shudder and we knew that our guest couldn't leave. Mother said, "Miss Leigh, you must spend the night here, the storm may go on till morning. I'll telephone to your friends." But the wires were down, so mother said, "It doesn't matter. They'll know you're safe with us."

Our guest room was on the ground floor, and as mother was showing it to her I heard Audrey Leigh say, "Oh dear, I'm terribly afraid of lightning, I'm afraid I shan't be able to sleep." And then mother said, "Margaret, why don't you sleep down here with Miss Leigh? Then neither of you will be afraid."

There was a little silence, then the lovely voice said, "Oh yes, do, I shall be so comforted."

My heart and all things stood still . . .

What had happened? Nothing had happened, but something immense, something unimaginable was taking place. Did mother realize what she had said? It was as if some unknowable situation were opening before me, some consequence announced, and weighed; something portentous, and yet at the same time redolent with a more exquisite happiness than anyone had ever known.

We dined, and as the evening and the storm went on I kept *feeling* and thinking, "What *am* I *feeling?*" I knew that I was experiencing a rapture too mysterious to be understood; it was like music — far, far beyond life. One didn't try to explain such mysteries, they were inexpressible. "I shall be so comforted". . . In the space of a few seconds I felt that I had lived a full lifetime of experience, and suddenly knew all there was to know about love.

Everyone was eating and drinking and talking, but I was living. All the others except Audrey Leigh had disappeared, like the people and objects on the darkened porch. Seated in her circle of light, she alone existed — and she was visible only to me. Our communication was secret and complete, and consisted of one essential word: "Ah?"

When I came downstairs to the guest room she was already in bed. The dressing-table held perfumes and powders in profusion, and the maid had brought nightgowns and negligées for her to choose from. She lay wrapped in a glow of amethyst and candlelight.

Her face was in shadow, but I felt her compelling eyes on me. "Are you frightened?" she asked, and I said "No."

She said nothing more. I blew out the candles and lay down beside her. I tried to say something inconsequent, but she didn't answer. Waves of emotions engulfed me. I wasn't questioning or puzzled, I was overcome with ecstasy. In silence we listened to the storm; in silence I felt that I was listening to the vibrations of her presence, of her life. Finally she turned toward me and in a flash of lightning I saw that her eyes had deepened. For an instant I felt her fragrant face against my cheek. "Lovely one," she said, "goodnight." And she touched her lips softly to mine.

All night I lay awake, held motionless in an infinite seduction. When lightning illuminated the room I tried to see her face again. If she too were awake, had she been looking at me? If so, her eyes had closed before I could be certain. Was she conscious of what I was feeling? Was it possible that she shared this strange and turbulent enchantment? Then I realized that she was sleeping.

Toward morning I too fell asleep. And when I wakened she had already dressed and left the room. The sun was shining. The amethyst gown and negligée lay over a chair.

She stayed two more days at the lake and I saw her once. Her friends gave a party for her, and as she moved about among them she talked with mother and the others but made no gesture toward me, though at moments I thought I saw her eyes turn in my direction. At last I went to speak to her, but I was puzzled and hurt because her manner was withdrawn, almost as if she didn't know me, as if no miracle had occurred. I felt thrust back into the world I had lived in "before." We were still exchanging words like strangers when someone called to her. She didn't seem to hear, so I put my hand on her arm. I made the gesture without thinking, and no one could have been more surprised than I was at the vibration that shot through my fingers — an electrical voltage as if I had touched a live wire. Gently withdrawing her arm, she gave me her hand, smiling and saying, "It's been charming." Then she moved away, disappearing from me into the world of people and teacups, words and gestures. I left the party and went back to my room in the cottage where I could think and try to discover what had happened, why and wherefore and therefore . . . what I must do.

The next day I was still in such a paralysis of emotion that I walked for hours, without even thinking of trying to see her again. I would wait until I could decide what to do; I didn't know until the day after that she was leaving for New York and London. Which she did, without a sign or a word.

— 2 —

After this shock, life was like death to me.
Why had she been different? What had become of the
miracle? It had existed from the first moment I saw her; she too
had felt it, she had let me see that she recognized it, she
couldn't deny that it had happened. So what was I to do now
without it? I would have to go to London . . .

At eighteen, what does one know? Everything and nothing.
But "everything" becomes distorted later; one has to fight for the
everything that one began with.

I began by quickly accepting the fact that what had
happened to me wasn't the kind of thing that happened to
other people. Boys fell in love with girls, girls fell in love with
boys, but for some reason I *didn't* fall in love with boys. This
was something I had always known, but never thought about.
Boys were prevalent, but none of them could ever make me fall
in love. They were hard and strong, they were unattractive, they
had ugly muscles and rough skins and no faint trace of charm.
What could they know about drowning in charm, as I was now
doing? How could girls find anything in boys to compare with
this rapture? How strange girls were, not to be like me! It never
occurred to me that *I* was "strange"; I was merely different, had
been born different. So much the better. I even thought for a
long time that I was the only person in the world made in my
image.

And even in later years, when I knew boys with beautiful
faces and muscles, my feeling never changed. Once, in France,
I saw a boy of such startling beauty walking over a bridge in
Perpignan that I turned the car and followed him for a long
time, gazing at his face and rhythmic walk as if I could never
absorb enough of such perfection. But to have related this

aesthetic emotion to a personal one — to imagine being love with him — never, never could it be.

I had fallen in love with a face, with an emanation; for the first time my heart had been shaken by a human discovery that was like my long-ago discovery of the meaning of music. Years later, in Paris, I watched an artist's intense face as he tried to describe the moment in his youth when he had discovered Proportion. He was so concentrated in trying to find words for his sudden insight that I had never forgotten what he said. And now I had had a comparable experience: a face, a voice, a vision of overwhelming beauty . . . she had become for me love in all its madness, and every other emotion vanished from the world.

In my desolation I could endure no one else, and no one, it seemed, could endure me. I didn't know what parents, sisters, friends, thought of my state, what plight they imagined I was in. They had ceased to exist for me; everything ceased — nature no longer held magic, days and hours no longer led me toward infinite delights, only music still had power. All I could think of for months, all I could accept from life as worthy of acceptance, was my need to be charmed. Charm became for me a voracious appetite.

Until I saw her again, how could I go on living? And if I never saw her again, what would become of my life? If I found her, what mystery would it lead to? If I never found her, whom would I find who could produce such a miracle of adoration? A boy? Such a suggestion would have astounded me if anyone had ever offered it, but no one did. Perhaps I would find another fabulous apparition from some unknown world? I didn't believe it . . . no one could compare with her. And the truth is that, when I came to know her, her qualities surpassed even those I had first sensed in her. No one else knew how to talk about love, how to write about love, how to *be* in love, as she did.

I didn't of course talk to my parents about what had happened. They lived in a world far removed from mine, which their imaginations would never help them to understand. But to everyone else I could talk, and did, never suspecting that they might not understand me either. I always began by saying, "Oh, if you only knew!" — as if all that I felt and knew wasn't at the disposition of anyone else. I was spared any need to defend my position by my ignorance of how people might judge it. If I had ever felt the guilt and isolation which I was later to read about as stigmatizing this "sharper love," I would have fought to the death for my authentic right to it. As it was, this occasion never arose. My conviction of possessing personal authority was so rooted that I continued to pursue my life as if no one would ever dare to criticize me about anything. And in fact no one ever did . . . I mean, only one person did. And that was she.

Autumn came to the lake, poplar leaves fell in flurries of gold, and sadness was in the air. September came. I had to go back to college, but I was still under such intoxication that even the hatred of returning to an institution of learning had little reality to me.

How drab everyone and everything there appeared to my new eyes and sensibilities. Had these college girls never heard of love? Were they all — even the attractive ones — untouched by all that I had become aware of?

And then one day a rumor ran through the corridors and the campus — a story to be talked of only in whispers . . . the story of a girl, a junior, who had a "crush" on one of the teachers. Her family had become alarmed because she had begged to stay on in college during the vacations, when the teacher was there; they didn't want her to return for her senior year, and she had begun to "pine away." The teacher was a mouse-like creature whom no one could possibly associate with love — or so I thought. But even the family doctor could prescribe nothing for the girl's "anemia" but to send her back to college, where the menace to her health would be less than if she were deprived of the beloved presence.

The rumor persisted, but the girl returned. I think no one quite believed in the somber repercussions of the story. We speculated about it for weeks, in the vague excitement created by ignorance, but finally the gossip died. I remember no talk of penalties or consequences.

And then, before the end of the year, I was surprised to find myself falling in love. It was merely an episode, nebulous and uncommitted, a substitute experience — no betrayal of my allegiance to the fabulous face, the mythical essence lost to me somewhere in London. It came about through a blend of music and love, since the attractive junior — who at first awed me and then seemed to cherish me — was a musician who played the piano with a haunting talent. This furnished all the spring days and nights with the required exaltations, and college became a temple for me. There was a balcony under the stars where I sat, night after night, listening to strains of Schumann, Chopin, Liszt, Mendelssohn pouring out over the moonlit campus . . .

Her presence made another year of college bearable, but when she graduated I refused to go on with the academic boredom I loathed. I had decided to face and force the world, manage somehow to get to New York and start a career, equip myself for the great impetus which would one day take me to London and to *her*. I made these plans with a confidence that seems fictional to me today. I was sure that my resolution would never falter, and confident that its fulfillment would be all that I planned it to be.

I did finally get to New York — I scarcely remember how — and three intense years flew by: a job in a publisher's office, reviewing books, reading and editing manuscripts. I was happy too. Every morning dawned for me like a morning in May, with vistas of enchantment at the end of every path through the spring woods. And it wasn't long before I discovered, for the first time, the "reality" of love. But it was a reality that failed to turn into a dream; therefore it wasn't what I was seeking. It was an artless, natural, explicit experience — so simple that it could create no spell for me. Even at its height I could only contrast it with what it could have been, if only . . .

One of my friends from the lake had also found a job in New York, and it was through her — after nearly five years — that my dream began to form again. She was a friend of the friends who had brought Audrey Leigh to tea on that faraway afternoon, and it was she who telephoned me, one day in

October, to announce in an excited voice: "She's coming to New York to spend the winter!"

Thus it was in New York, and not in London, that Audrey Leigh appeared in my life once more.

— 3 —

It was over a tea table at the Plaza that Audrey Leigh and I began the friendship which, at intervals, was to magnetize my life for thirty years.

We had met a few days before, as if by chance, in the flat of her New York friends. But behind the chance there had been careful planning on my part, and when I walked into the apartment high up in the New York sky, across from the Plaza, and saw her holding court to people and friends, I felt again that she existed apart from them, and that they all gravitated around her.

As soon as she saw me she stopped talking, rose and came to greet me. "You!" she said — "I've so often remembered you."

This time there was no withdrawal in her; on the contrary she seemed to emerge from boredom to give me a special welcome. I was five years older than when I had first seen her, and had gained a measure of assurance. "I couldn't resist trying to see you again," I said. "I've always wanted to."

"Really?" she said. "I'm very flattered."

She introduced me to her friends, at whom I don't remember looking; and when, finally, I rose to go, she walked with me to the door, murmuring in her muted voice, "You must have tea with me one day."

My lake-friend reported later, "She thinks you're charming — so un-American. She says she'd take you to Buckingham Palace with her any day."

From the first I felt a special light and freedom around us, within us, ahead of us. Between us there was an extraordinary ease, swift communication, facility of words, delighted and delightful laughter; and there was no barrier of generation — we were so attuned that we almost never had to finish a sentence or the end of a thought, each knew at once that the other's contribution would lead to the pleasure of agreement, the stimulation of humor, the excitement of victory or capitulation which follows opposition.

We met often and the first thing I learned about her was what no one had thought to tell me — that she wasn't English. She had been born in New York, but when she was twenty-five had gone to London and had loved it so much that she decided to make her home there. "It is civilization," she said. "The English are gentle people. I couldn't live in America — everyone here is so forthright." She had later become a British subject.

My special delight in our communication was the reward of finding myself in a world more subtle than the one in which I had been born. How I had longed for this transposition! Audrey Leigh was the first person with whom I could talk about all those things the people I knew didn't talk about. Finesse in any realm was without interest in my parents' world — an unknown quality. Behavior was evaluated as right or wrong, "nice" or not nice — not beautiful and attractive as against awkward and inexpressive; general ideas weren't subjects of conversation; literature, art, music weren't discussed — music was listened to, not talked about; impact of mind upon mind was unsolicited, unneeded. My friends had no enthusiasm for a thousand discriminations which I wanted upheld in a thousand realms. I longed to read the books they never read; I longed for more sensitive standards of taste, for passionate arguments about what was beautiful and what wasn't, for excitement about good looks, good clothes, about beautiful hands and eyes and noses, beautiful smiles, ways of talking, accents, tones of voice, ways of walking and standing and sitting — all the minutiae that make for the embellishment of life; but around me I heard only the flat, monotonous, pedestrian, domestic ramblings of everyday interests and occupations and thoughts.

With Audrey Leigh all was suave and perceptive. What discernment, what discrimination she had in all her swift

43

judgments! "How do you always know so exactly what is the best, the most fitting?" I asked her — "how everyone should dress, do one's hair, emphasize one's type? You always seem to know at a glance."

"I love it that you do too," she said.

She talked much about her friends. The ones she valued most appeared to be those statesmen she knew in Parliament whose limpid prose speech she so admired, as she admired London and all the ways of English life. She had been brought up by governesses and regretted that she hadn't had a classical education. But she had a sure instinct for great prose, and an infallible judgment of whether a poem had the substance that made it major rather than minor. In all these matters we were allied.

As to her relations with people, she "held no brief except for genius." Her idea of the subtleties of human intercourse couldn't have been more autocratic, and it was this splendid prerogative that kept me in an exhilarated state of challenge — would she approve or condemn? I felt that I was living on tiptoe, prepared to meet any contest or scrutiny. I became a different person, one I had never had a chance to be before.

Of course we had soon talked of our meeting at the lake, and one day I asked, "I wonder if you have any idea of the impression you first made on me?"

"Why not?" she said, smiling at me with closest tenderness.

"But why did you?" I persisted.

She waited, and then answered as if she were preparing me for a situation I might find unpleasant. "But I have so often known it," she said.

And so my jealousy began, and my determination to make myself more than an episode to her. "Audrey," I said — "the most beautiful name in the world, except Helen. 'Audrey, thy beauty is to me' " . . .

What mockery, what sweetness, there was in her laughter; in her manner — invitation and remoteness, promise and withdrawal, advance and reserve. She's more adorned than other women, I thought. She really is like a great actress, I said later, after I had seen Bernhardt. Sarah never portrayed nature unaided; her heroines were always presented as women who knew how, with art, to present their natures. This knowledge was Audrey Leigh's art in life. How often I said to myself, feeling that I was speaking aloud, "I cannot live unless I can spend my time with you; there is no one else who knows how to act, to speak, to smile, to *be*, except you."

It seemed to me that she never breathed or moved, smiled or spoke, paused in the middle of a phrase or deliberately failed to finish it, without increasing my enchantment. And she had a way of veiling all direct statements that gave them an allurement beyond their content. She would never say, for instance, "The train leaves immediately"; it gave her some exquisite pleasure to say, "The train leaves almost at once." She loved a double negative; she would never say, "He was a cad" — she preferred to put it, "He was not sufficiently unlike a cad." In a note to me one day she wrote, "I fain would see you, but . . ." and this archaism delighted me most of all. She loved to begin a sentence with "I must not, I dare not say . . ." All that was not totally committed was rewarding to her.

And there was authority in her — she could be as dominant as she was seductive. This combination gave me a satisfaction of which I never tired.

Why were these nuances so necessary to me, a product of American life at its most rapid and direct? No one I knew placed a value on them — my contemporaries only laughed at my enthusiasms. But their mocking questions gave me the excitement of definition, of argument; pushed my mind and its passion for discrimination to a fierce effort at persuasion.

"You're crazy," my friends said. But they judged me crazy about so many things that the word was as meaningless to them as it was to me.

One day we were having tea at the Waldorf — the old Waldorf in which one wandered as through botanical gardens. Something she said, as her hands made a ceremony among the tea things, produced again that black-out I had experienced the first day we met: the room turned dark and I saw only her hands lighted by a search-light. As if hypnotized by her large topaz ring, I felt myself leave the world of reality and speak as I would in a world of dream. "Oh," I said, "I adore you, I adore you."

She said nothing, she seemed to enter a silence as remote from reality as my own. Then, as she raised her eyes heavily to mine, a wave passed across her features, almost obliterating them, and she spoke in a voice I had never heard before.

"Darling," she said, "you mustn't say it . . . you mustn't."

I don't remember leaving the Waldorf, I remember only our walking up Fifth Avenue, talking as if nothing had happened.

— 4 —

From that day, however, there was an almost imperceptible change in her. The great ease between us lessened; she erected a psychic barrier over which I was too inexperienced to leap. The change wasn't in her voice, or in her words, so much as in her manner: I never again had the sensation that, when she left a phrase unfinished, it was because she meant you to feel she had finished it by gathering you to her heart.

And then one day when I met her at the Plaza for lunch, she stood silent and hard before my greeting, saying simply, "I want to talk with you." She walked quickly into the dining room without another word.

Our table was in a secluded corner, and after we had ordered our luncheon she waited a long moment before speaking. When she finally broke the silence, it was with hesitation and difficulty.

"Margaret," she said, "I must ask you something . . ."

I waited, since she seemed unable to go on.

"And you must answer me truthfully."

"Of course," I said — "answer what?"

"Tell me" . . . She still hesitated. Her face was closed and she refused to look at me. "Are you — it's difficult to say" . . .

"But what?" I asked again — "am I *what?*" I couldn't imagine what she was talking about. "What do you want to ask me?"

"Are you — oh, I can't say it."

In a flash — I don't know why — I realized what was coming. I had no complicated feelings about it; why not be quite simple and direct? So I said, "Are you trying to ask me if I'm a lesbian?"

"Don't say it, don't say it — it's horrible."

"What's horrible about it?" I said. I felt very calm and cold. "I thought of course you knew."

"I've tried not to know."

"But I've always been," I said — "I couldn't be anything else. Why are you thinking about it now?"

"People have been talking."

Her distress seemed real, yet for the first time I had the impression that she was behaving unlike her real self with me.

"I don't understand why it distresses you," I said. "Is there anything flagrant about me?"

"Oh no, no," she said. "No one would ever dream . . . You are like a flower."

After this the dark subject was always in the foreground. I couldn't resist matching my wits with hers, and always felt that I came out the victor.

"You've read the wrong books," I said. "I've never had that absurd 'Well of Loneliness' feeling of isolation and guilt — it seems tragic and unnecessary to me. I was born to be what I am. Is it my fault that I can love only what I love?"

"But it's against nature."

"Anything that is in Nature is nature," I said. She set her face against me, but I went on. "*I* like men, I have many men friends. But I couldn't be in love with them. It's as inconceivable to me as that I should ever be a mother."

"Oh, do stop saying such awful things — I can't bear it."

I was silent, watching her across the table. She brushed aside a waiter. "There is a well-known woman in London who is noted for such *moeurs**. I knew her years ago, and I knew a girl who was in love with her. When I talked with the girl she had nothing to say, she simply hid her face in her hands."

"She must have been a very ordinary sort of girl," I said. "I'm not that kind of person."

"You don't yet know what you are, you've had no experience of the world."

---

*inclinations

"I'm not interested in 'the world,'" I said. "I'm interested in love, and what I can make of it; and I know that no one knows as much about it as you do — I don't care what you say."

"Oh yes, I know about it," she said . . . "too much about it." She spoke in a new flat voice. "Years ago, after I had married, I fell deliriously in love with a man who was also married. We took things into our own hands, we went away together — we fled to India, we went everywhere — it was 'the world well lost.' But it became such a physical obsession that I couldn't go on with it — I knew that my life was being swamped in the physical, and I knew that I couldn't live indefinitely like that." She raised her eyes, dark with memories. "There never has been such a lover."

I reached for my glass, but couldn't raise my arm. It had become iron.

"I finally left him," she went on. "He died a year later. It has always been on my conscience. Even a normal passion can be soul-destroying, and as for what everyone knows to be abnormal . . ."

I was aghast. I began at once to plan a campaign, with the aid of Havelock Ellis and Krafft-Ebing, against such ignorant judgments of "normal" and "abnormal."

Unconscious of my thoughts, she began to tell me how, after her "immoral" love, she had had a religious conversion and had given herself over to "good works" in London ever since.

"And love?" I asked,

"I have put it out of my life. My husband is still living. 'Thou shalt not commit adultery.' I had a choice, and I made it. I believe that one should live by Christ's laws."

"But you're not the kind of person to live without love. It's a denial of life, it's ghastly. Don't you really think so?"

"Oh, dearest one," she said, "do you seriously expect me to give any answer?"

"Yes," I said, "I do. You can't really believe that there's anything *wrong* about my having fallen so wonderfully in love with you? Why would it happen if it were wrong? Is this what people mean when they talk about 'original sin'? Surely you don't believe in such a silly idea! I fall in love, I have the most beautiful emotions one can have, and am I supposed to listen calmly when I'm told that I shouldn't have them? No one can take them from me — I *have* them, they *came* to me, why should I distrust them? I couldn't deny them, they exist, they are *true*. You have a beautiful face, this is *true* — shall I try to convince myself that your face is ugly? I'm beginning to think that something wrong is going on in the world, but it's not going to go on in me!"

"The world knows there's something wrong about this kind of love . . ."

"Then why did it happen to me? Am I a person to whom wrong things happen? Why should they?"

"Darling, you can't fight the world."

"I can if I have to."

"But — don't you see? You talk as if you defied the whole human race."

"Oh," I said lightly, with despair, "I've never really felt that I belong to the human race."

That love could be evil was to me an idea as grotesque as believing that it could be sinful to write a symphony. We argued aridly about it, and enchantment disappeared from the world.

All our consequent meetings were dedicated to conflict. Religion dominated our conversations, and I had to listen to ideas which extol God as made in the image of man. These ideas embarrassed me to the point of revulsion. I thought they belonged to the dark ages, I was sure that intelligent people had stopped thinking in terms of a personal God, of an orthodox Heaven and Hell, of Good and Evil as evaluated by the staggering childishness of evangelists and theologians. I was having my first revelation of what I was to understand much later — the havoc that is created in people, the deformations of their lives and characters by those misty ideas from which they draw their concepts of religion. I began to feel maddened, and as we continued to argue I often wondered whether, had I possessed the dialectical genius of a Socrates, I could have convinced Audrey Leigh of the sublimity of any faith but her own. I gave up all hope, not only because I lacked the Socratic gift, but because I felt that no one could combat the combination of confusion and conviction that made up her beliefs — after all, Socrates had an audience of orderly minds. *Her* mind was incapable of following an argument; she never knew when a point had been scored. Even when I won a debate — as I was always doing — what good would it ever do, since she was oblivious to my victory? Nevertheless, even without hope, I struggled on through the maze of pointless discussion. It was like struggling with a jellyfish — she slid away and slithered back again to her original position.

If I tried to prove that human love, on its plane, was a counterpart of love on a higher plane, and that the senses should be honored in their own province, she would agree — enveloping me with all her charm. But in the next move, changing to grimness, she would relate all physical love — except in marriage — to evil.

She believed what she said, and I was only twenty-three. Oh, I knew that there were profound things to be said, and that the churches didn't say them, and sometimes I thought my mind would break if I couldn't find a way to make them clear.

What had happened to the love I had been feeling in her, from her, until the Being she called God had decreed that it was evil?

Absorbed in my efforts to produce new arguments, I didn't realize that the time had come for her return to London, and she managed to slip away without seeing me again, leaving only a letter of farewell: "Listen to the words my heart is saying, and let them bring a lovely healing for any pain my coming may have brought to you."

I continued to live through the next months. I had done what I could to destroy non-destructible attitudes, sometimes struggling patiently, sometimes battling my way, sometimes using my mind with what I believed was devastating clarity and persuasiveness, sometimes becoming stupefied over my own (so unexpected) stupidities, and sometimes suffering the almost

The Middle

— 1 —

Un être vous manque, et le monde est dépeuplé . . ."*
Once again I wandered through an empty world. The old-fashioned conflicts over religion into which I had been snared remained inconceivable to me. Yet they had the quality of nearly all human conflicts: superfluous but unavoidable, demanding as much courage, wasting as much energy, as if they were inevitable.

Under my anguish I had been growing up and was thus ready for a great event when it came. It appeared in the form of two new friends, and if I were allowed a single phrase to indicate what inspiration they offered me I would say: a complete life-education.

I shan't use their real names. Though both of them are dead, one of them (American) would have objected. The other (French) wouldn't have minded in the least, would in fact have found it interesting and amusing to be named. Being an expert in satirizing *les bêtises humaines,* she never refused the opportunity to observe and criticize herself as she played her part, like everyone else, in these grotesqueries which compose what we call *la comédie humaine.* One of the first things I heard her say was: *"Helas! jamais le génie n'égalera l'abondance, la continuité, l'imprévu de la bêtise!"*†

But this French friendship came later, after I had met the extraordinary American whom I shall call Kaye. We embarked on a literary companionship which was to last until she died, and which brought humor and vitality into my personal history. Kaye was too human to be defined merely as an intellectual, and she

---

*"One person is absent, and the world is unpeopled . . ."
†Loosely translated: "Alas! never will the spirit be a match for the everlasting abundance and surprise of human stupidity!" — Ed.

55

had a vigor that balanced what she called my "mistiness." I loved her sardonic bite and attack, especially her laughter — but such warm laughter! — over my romantic tragedy.

"Buckingham Palace!" she snorted. "Tell her you'll be glad to go with her if she happens to be going the same day you are."

— 2 —

For four years, in New York, Kaye and I spent our time making life "beautiful" — no concessions to the usual, the sensible, the easily-attained; no limits to the possible. All was joy, art, effort, work, obsession with the mind and its powers, the discovery and mystery of genius — the kind of life I had always longed for, as different from ordinary existence as a flower is from a weed. We expressed all this effervescence in a magazine of the arts. Of course we were only doing what the inspired young have always done, but doing it, I thought, with greater intensity and more lustrous success.

As for my personal contribution to this exceptional life, I never stopped talking about "beauty." Why did I feel that it was my function to go to war for beauty? I used the noun so continuously that I often saw people looking at me with annoyance or pity, sometimes with revulsion. In our Greenwich Village evenings with friends, I would become impatient when Kaye — despite my urgings — refused to be lured into her most brilliant talk; and since the too-human, too-unaesthetic musings of the others bored me I would withdraw to a far corner of the room beside the victrola, my head bent close to the sounding-board, as I turned the crank and played over and over a record of Debussy's "Faun." These were my moments of the ecstasy of life, and though outsiders would have been happy to ridicule me, my friends never did. Naturally I believed, with Blake, that excess leads to wisdom.

My private world, too, now had a new motive for excess — a correspondence with Audrey Leigh which had begun slowly, after her return to London, and had continued through the years with a mounting accretion; letters which established a new beginning, as if we had never been estranged. At first conventional in tone, they had finally become more personal, and they were embodied in a handwriting so striking, so evidently designed as a calligraphic art, that they should have been photographed.

If anyone had asked me what kind of letters would have the power to enchant me utterly, I would have answered, "Those I am now receiving." I read with rapture sentences like, "Do know all that I do not tell you here"; or, "If I began to say personal things to you, could I stop? Do urge me to begin." There was one that I repeated to myself over and over: "I have longed to talk with you — shall I say all the hours of all the days?" Who but she knew how to offer such exquisite tentatives? I felt as if my nature was being manipulated by an expert.

As time went on she drew nearer and nearer. "Can you follow my days, have you heard my thoughts? Dare I hope for so complete an understanding — a companionship so radiantly satisfying?" In another, "I think of you days — hours — minutes"; and, "Darling, I see you so clearly — and constantly. Have you felt how intensely my thoughts have been trying to attract the aroma and allure of your spirit?" Then there came a phrase that I treasured above all: "And now I must begin to say goodnight to you . . ."

"Bravo!" laughed Kaye. "A hand on the exact octave that is you!"

Through all my bedazzlement I retained enough common sense to share Kaye's laughter, but it was her understanding of my state that filled me with gratitude. In reality I was so enfolded in the aesthetic euphoria produced by these letters — it was so total, and seemed to me so unaccountable — that it created in me a secret life, stronger than anything that took place in the life around me.

At last the word "love" made its appearance in the beautiful handwriting. "You will rest in the absolute assurance that there is only love in my heart. You may always know it." And then, "Goodnight — oh, goodnight, and again and again and yet again . . . but I may not write a line more except to say I love you."

I was overwhelmed. I kept saying to myself, "This really sounds to me like love." To have brought such a response, I decided that my letters must have been more effective than I imagined, must have held some magic of which I was unconscious. Sometimes in a crowd I would find myself smiling at my future, as at a private heaven unattainable by others. I was sustained, protected, happy beyond other mortals, and convinced that I was building a relationship for the upper realms of life, the universe of romantic love.

— 3 —

The next blessing that a kind fate held in store for me was a new love — the love of a country, an old and mythical country in which, as it turned out, I was to live for the rest of my life.

For years, whenever I heard people talking about France, I had felt a thrill of nostalgia for this luminous country I had never seen. It was as if I knew in advance that Paris would be for me, as it had been for George Moore, "that white city to which we all come as beggars."

Kaye knew Paris well, had even lived there, and regarded it as the world's magical city. Therefore she agreed entirely with my idea that we should one day adopt it as our own. We began making plans to go — the kind of plans that are so wild, so intricate, and so difficult that one can't remember them afterward, or even remember how one had the courage to attempt them. But after a year's struggle — and just four years after Kaye and I had met — we were ready to leave New York. At last, one wonderful day, we stood on the deck of a ship — two beggars on their way to Le Havre . . . and the white city.

And Paris was not far from London.

The first time I saw Paris! . . . This, I thought, is the city where I belong, where I should have been born. I was at last to know patriotism, which had always been only a word to me.

The sanctuary of France . . . what was the protection it offered? What was its promise? "Rescued" was the word I repeated most often as Kaye and I walked the streets of Paris

60

and drank in the sights and sounds of the unbelievable city. The sudden beauty of a balcony's grillwork, a faultless building, the courtyard gardens, the winding Seine, the sense of light and freedom . . .

Rescued from *what*, rescued *for* what? Rescued from sameness, from the regulated, the dull, the alien, the arid, the incomplete, the inarticulate, from what Henry James called "the whimsical retention of speech which is such a common form of American sociability." And for what? First of all for leisured living, for the cult of beauty, for the civilized, for give and take, for the culture that could always be taken for granted, for native brilliance and wit, for the gaiety that rests on seriousness, for the Gallic value that is placed on grace of manner.

The gods who were still directing my destiny produced the next miracle. I was taken by some English friends to a small left-bank theater where a famous *diseuse* (singer, actress, writer) was talking about the new French poets. Afterward we went to her flat in the rue Barbet de Jouy, near the Musée Rodin, and it was on this night of poetry that the great friendship of my life had its beginning.

My first impression of Claire Lescaut was that she possessed some special human inspiration, some illumination, that was a mystery which only time and knowledge would help me to understand. This quality was so evident that one almost stopped thinking of how beautiful her face was; I found that I was responding above all to the touching charm in which her personality was enveloped — a personality, I felt, of such strength and sweetness that it could only be founded on some great purity of nature.

When the *soirée* ended and we left her flat, I searched for words to express the emotions I had been feeling. The only ones I found were these: "She is like a stronghold." Trust in the purity of a nature . . . this is the quality which was to lead to a deathless love.

She spoke no English, and my college French was pitiable; I

could scarcely remember a word of the language I was supposed to have learned. However, I was determined to communicate, so I invented a language that existed somewhere above the rational world but which Claire Lescaut could understand. Though she was as well-known for the grace of her prose as for her exquisite diction, she was no pedant, and she was so entertained by my non-grammar (I always spoke in the present tense) and my incredible accent that she refused to correct me. It wasn't long before I was able to talk about Freud (then in great vogue) in a French that was primitive but clear.

"What I like about Americans," Claire told me, " is their instant ability to show their enthusiasm, and their disarming frankness in presenting their personalities. We are old and formal, we are always polite, we are *plutôt* reserved, so we respond to the way Americans are so immediately able to reveal their inner lives." And she added, "The Russians have the same talent."

As one always does in France, we talked a great deal about beauty. One of my English friends was irritated by the French mania for speaking of beauty before other qualities. "Don't they ever think of anything else?" she said. "I think it's silly to put so much emphasis on how people look, rather than on what they are."

"Tell her," Claire said, "that we speak of it first because it is the first observation that can be honestly made — the visual. It would be pretentious to speculate, at once, on someone's inner life. That becomes visible soon afterward, through a hundred little revelations. But beauty has such importance, physically as well as psychically. How can anyone be insensitive to it, or untrained to recognize it? Ah, the English!"

It wasn't long before I told her about my arrested adolescent experience of romantic love. How sympathetic she was, how amused, how informed. "But you must see her again," she said. "Perhaps she will be kinder to you next time."

Ah, I thought, *this* is civilization: life as it is, simply and really, no matter in what realm; no inhibitions, no need for

Freud, no self-consciousness, no stoppages. "You will achieve what you are able to inspire," Claire went on. "But you must know how to proceed, you must learn the value of *prélude*. Naïveté won't help you, or candor, or simplicity — except with people who are highly organized. In this case you must learn to understand nineteenth-century England."

I discovered that in France nothing that was genuine in human experience was outlawed; nothing was discounted — at least in the artist milieu — except the uneasy, the strained, the unknowing, the bourgeois. And the French attitude toward sex eased my emotional tensions. No one was shocked by sex classifications — they spoke of *pédérastes* without any of the American leer at "fairies" or "pansies"; they looked upon lesbians as a race of charming people. These tendencies were not regarded as aberrations but as non-conformities; the unusual, the rare — perhaps the unaccountable; singular, but not abnormal; anomalous, perhaps, but original; in any case, exceptional and interesting.

"Androgynous," Claire said. "Your Audrey should have understood."

"But the word 'androgyne' isn't in common usage in America," I said. "Americans don't discuss these differentiations; they talk only of 'normal' sex; for sex variations they have only contempt, pity, hatred or ribaldry."

France had André Gide and others who wrote frankly about their natures. But though the French bourgeois tended to loathe such types, you could always talk with him easily about them as you couldn't with bourgeois Americans. Claire even told me that the subject was sometimes discussed in public debate: a well-known American ex-patriate, seconded by a titled French-woman, had defended lesbianism on the lecture platform without causing the slightest scandal.

I was intrigued by the story about Verlaine who, always in financial difficulties, was urged by friends to ask for governmental assistance. He wrote to the Président du Conseil:

"Je suis pauvre, je suis poète, je suis pédéraste" . . . considering that the last qualification was sure to draw sympathetic attention to his difficulties. And I became quite used to Frenchwomen who, when they wanted to advertise their love affairs, said to you proudly, *"Oui, je suis Vénusienne."*

"No one talks like this in America," was all I could say. "It's a rest for the mind and its superfluous conflicts."

---

*"I am poor, I am a poet, I am a pederast."

— 4 —

In the summer when Claire left her Paris flat she lived in a romantic old château, in a forest, where lonely birds sang at twilight and three poplar trees, standing side by side, waved gently all day in the bright air. The forest formed a circle around the château-pavillon, and hundreds of chestnut trees enclosed you in their green and white shade, or their autumn gold. On nights of cold moonlight, deer approached the poplar trees with delicate steps and held midnight revels as if dancing to an inaudible music. In winter a ring of rain encircled the beautiful old dwelling, and great logs flamed in the Louis XIV fireplaces; in spring, on May mornings, a cuckoo sang through the early hours; and in late summer there was a stillness of sun and dusk that prepared you slowly for the coming solstice.

It was here that Claire lived like Armide* in her enchanted gardens and received her friends. Kaye and I were now counted among them, and spent long week-ends in the château, wandering through the forest, improving our French in the laziest way — by being forced to speak it — and enjoying the freedom of French hospitality as offered by an artist. The château contained several guest-suites where one could live as privately as *chez soi*.

In the concentrated romanticism of this *mise en scène* and its romantic châtelaine I felt that my life had arrived at its zenith. A wand had been waved and I was where I should be, when I should be — in the old world of France, where the art and science of love are discussed with a seriousness and a literacy not be found in the country of my birth.

And, now that I was near England, Audrey Leigh was more

---

*Armide — romantic heroine of Gluck's 1777 lyric tragedy *Armide*.

than ever in my mind. Therefore it was natural that our correspondence should flower, that we should even write of seeing each other, here or in London. Under Claire's tutelage my letters had sounded a new impersonal note — the tonality suited to what she called a prelude. And this effort at detachment had received an instant response.

The dreaded word "lesbianism" no longer seemed to exist; perhaps she had even forgotten that such an issue had ever divided us?

This was the epoch of leisure for letter-writing. One could put one's extra life into letters, expressing all that would never have been expressed in the unleisured momentum of daily living . . . conversations that could be wandered into instead of walked into directly. Time was needed to build such a relationship, and all my efforts at correspondence were focused to attract that special prose of endearments barely expressed which was so irresistible to me.

"I know that your thoughts are mine at times," she wrote — "I do not even pretend to guess what they are. Yet I would be happier if I felt that you knew my mind, my heart." I took the letters into the forest and read them over and over.

Before a year had passed Kaye's work obliged her to move to London, and Claire invited me to live in her forest château.

This enchanted place became my home in France, and I doubt that many people in the world have known a greater happiness than I knew in this golden period. To live in an adored country, in the most elysian surroundings, with a most beloved friend . . . and, as an added blessing, perhaps a romantic love awaiting me.

Claire and I often talked about Audrey Leigh. "Why don't you invite her here?" she asked one day. "Wouldn't you enjoy that?"

"No," I said, "I wouldn't enjoy it. I would probably die of happiness."

So she came.

It was late August and the beginning of summer's silence — the silence that holds the heart still, as when one thinks of

Apollinaire's *"odeur du temps"* — "fragrance of the season." I drove her out from Paris, listening to impersonal but cherishing talk and maintaining my rôle of detached but fascinated observer, allowing no memory of our New York conflict to mar our new rapprochement.

The meeting of hostess and guest was felicitous — one so suave in the French manner, the other so skilled in the English reticence that barely suggests the strange secret life beneath; Audrey's silver chain playing its familiar music as she moved across the *rotonde* toward Claire; and Claire, rising from her book-laden table with the posture and gestures of years of accumulated grace.

We sat before an early autumn fire and had a French tea and talked of all things except ideas and ourselves. But such was the persuasion of Claire's presence that the conventional world of Audrey Leigh dissolved before it, and she said to me later that night, "Here one doesn't have to 'act'? How releasing!" I knew that she meant her surface, social acting; nothing would ever stop her "acting" in the presentation of her inner self — this was a celebration to which she invited you, solicited your recognition, or, not receiving it, turned away.

"I don't know when I have so immediately liked anyone as I do your Claire," she said . . . "a rare combination of great artist and great lady."

And Claire said afterward, "I understand completely, *chérie*. It's as if she had spent a lifetime doing daily exercises in charm."

For ten days the dazzling visit continued, bringing us always to a closer harmony. And since the forbidden subject was never mentioned, she began to introduce it herself.

One night, after driving along moonlit roads, we returned to the sleeping château, talking of the spell that France provides and the ivory-tower that Claire had built in the depths of her forest.

"Tell me," Audrey said, not looking at me in the moonlight, "why do you care for me as you do?"

"Oh, for one reason, because I know you have such genius for love. I'm sure no one ever had more"... and then I stopped, remembering my hard-learned lesson. "Surely you agree?"

She turned and held me against her for an instant. "I 'die daily,'" she said, and for the second time since I had known her, she touched her lips softly to mine.

We walked silently into the salon and said goodnight.

The visit ended and she went back to London.

First there came a letter to Claire — "I feel that I should write in golden ink," Audrey said, and signed herself in her best Victorian manner, "I am yours to command."

To me she wrote, "I must not, I dare not, say how sweet every hour you gave was to me. You have convinced me of many things, and I cherish them and the process."

A few days later she found a phrase to surpass all those she had ever written to me: "There has not been a moment of forgetfulness. I am radiant of heart, as if an elixir had been inserted into my food and sleep." "Radiant of heart!"... My own heart lived in such flights of delight that I can't recall her words today without a loss of breath.

And the power of her words was matched by the hypnotic power her handwriting had upon me. Of all the handwriting I have ever seen, hers was the most lyrical. It was like a face too beautiful to be true; it became a presence as existent, as vivid, as a human presence, as indelible as some master line-drawing, as haunting as some unforgettable landscape. Her envelopes were resplendent — the sweep of the M's were a ship's sails in a full wind.

That these envelopes passed through the heavy hands of a rural postman became a sacrilege; I took them from him as if my own hands could save them from desecration. Where had she sat as she inscribed those matchless M's? How had her hand looked, and felt, as she formed their contours? What had been her mood as she wrote words in the full knowledge of my reward in reading them, since she knew that the pleasure she took in composing them matched my own pleasure in the knowledge that she had composed them consciously?

... September mornings, and the postman on his bicycle riding through the forest toward the château ... In his worn and dirty sack lay the letter. He took it into his big rough hand and gave it to me as if it contained no magic formula. I looked at him with gratitude and hate, I carried the letter into the forest, walking carefully in order not to fall, or die, before I could open it, holding the envelope before me like an *objet d'art;* and when I had gazed at the handwriting long enough for my heart to stop its quick beating, only to feel it quicken again as I gazed at the stamps she had placed so exactly in the proper relation to the sweep of the handwriting — like those Chinese characters in red ink placed so consciously beside a landscape that they became an inevitable part of the whole design — I opened the letter. "It is after midnight, but I shall take this down to the postbox myself, the sooner to reach you and let you know all that these poor words do not say . . ."

Had she worn her silver chain as she walked down the stairs and crossed the street to her postbox? Had no one been there to listen to its cadence? How near had she been to imagining my picture of her descending the stairs? And as she mounted them and walked back into her drawing-room, filled with the flowers she had listed in her letter — "Russian violets, huge white violets, pink gladiolas, white orchids, mauve orchids, tuberoses" — did she herself see the picture she made among them? Did she think again of me as she must have thought when she wrote, ". . . and their fragrance brings you to me"? Did she feel as I would have felt had I been there, in that London drawing-room I had never seen? Had she the faintest idea of the love that consumed me — or was all this art and beauty of handwriting and words simply a reflex of the fact that she was more enamored of art than of life and as subconsciously subject as I was to its ascendancy?

These phantasms haunted my life, fed my heart, preoccupied my mind. The fact that no one but Claire understood my dazzlement, that it was a matter of commiseration to others — this made no difference to me. Her endorsement, her laughter, her comprehension of my need for such evocations — this was

— 5 —

If you were here tonight I would try to tell you what my heart has been saying" . . . and with these words I was invited to spend November in London, in that Portland Square flat where I had visualized her life being lived and her letters written.

Having been created, I was confident that the "radiance" would endure, that I was equipped to keep it alight.

Kaye was still in London, and, due to her skill in rôle-playing the meeting between her and Audrey had been a smooth and (to us) amusing success. Audrey had succumbed at once to Kaye's attitude of mock tenderness, teasing challenge, and soothing protection — "She is the kind of person one can trust" . . . and Kaye and I were almost ashamed at the ease with which human frailties can be manipulated. But gradually the atmosphere changed. The intensity of our ideas — of our "religion," really — began to replace our interest in prolonged manipulation, and, before we realized it, Audrey sensed real challenge in the air. This led her to reassert her own ideas, and from that moment the visit which was to have been a consolidation turned to sudden disaster before my startled eyes.

A man for whose teaching Kaye and I had the deepest reverence (whom we called by his last name, Douglas) was available for conversation. We had been planning where to meet him — at the Café Royal perhaps?

"Why not here?" Audrey asked. "We can have him for tea."

"But we're meeting to talk," Kaye said.

"We can talk over tea."

"No," I hastened to say, "no important talk can be had over tea."

"I don't understand," Audrey said.

"Impersonal talk," Kaye said. "It just doesn't happen with tea.

71

You know . . . greetings and all the other inanities. Afterward you can only talk from the top of your mind."

Arguments, antagonisms, disfavor . . . Nevertheless our meeting took place at the Café Royal, and lasted late into the night. We had hoped that Audrey wouldn't come, but she "longed to hear what could be discussed in public˙ that couldn't be discussed in one's home."

What was discussed was, fatally, the time-worn subject of Good and Evil. "The essential difference between good and evil," said Douglas, "is whether you use the 'energy' you were born with to develop yourself, or whether you let it die from inertia. At a certain level of development there exists an objective morality — that of conscious action."

Audrey bristled. "Thou shalt not kill, thou shalt not steal! Surely you don't deny that such actions are evil."

"A conscious man doesn't kill or steal," said Douglas. "But if you want to talk of murder on the subjective level, there are many kinds of murder — not only physical. And stealing? What about stealing another person's emanations? Vampirism."

To this she found no answer. So she switched to the subject that obsessed her. "Sex aberrations are evil!"

"What *are* sex aberrations?" asked Douglas. "To discuss these matters we must first agree on a precise vocabulary. As long as we remain undeveloped, our famous 'morality' (sex or any other) isn't worth much more than traffic laws, or police regulations. We drive on the left or the right side of the street according to the local code. Subjective morality isn't of much more importance than that."

The evening ended, as Kaye and I had foreseen, on a dismal note. All that I had gained through careful planning and evasion had been lost in a single evening.

And in the days that followed I had my second revelation of the change that a fanatical deformation of a religion can effect in the personality of its devotee. Whenever the subject was approached, all Audrey's suavity and gentleness left her. The words "good and evil," "God," "God's will," "sin," "repentance," "surrender," "redemption," turned her into a witch-burner. The face that could fuse into such luminous tenderness changed into a mask of set fury; the voice of the charmer became strident with rage.

"I don't understand it," I said. "What is there in religion that suddenly makes you look like a Chinese dragon?" Then, as quickly as she had put it on, she discarded the grimacing mask and allowed her personal magic to emerge again. But as long as the dragon was functioning, a decomposition seemed to take place in her brain, affecting even her speech which lost all its grace.

I became desperate. I thought of going back to France.

A day or two later I was horrified to hear her say, "I've listened to *your* ideas, now it's only fair that you listen to mine." And she proposed to invite a group of friends to discuss the question of good and evil on her own ground and in her own terms.

I telephoned Kaye. "Come and help. These will be people who believe that emotional conviction can win any argument. It will be grim."

"Leave me out of it," Kaye said. "You want a miracle. you want me to sit down in a chair, facing Audrey Leigh, and by talking for a few hours change her into an adult being. Such things can't be done."

"What can *I* do then?"

"Nothing. Protect yourself. Don't argue."

The talk that I couldn't avoid took place in Audrey's drawing-room. A dozen people came, and as I learned afterward, they all belonged to a religious organization called the Oxford Group.* It was evident at once that they knew why they had come and that they felt invincible. Their face-expressions were enjoying in advance my inevitable defeat.

After endless flutterings and chatterings Audrey announced that Mr. So-and-So would expose the common point of view. He exposed a great deal, all of it very common. I took him to be

---

*See Introduction, page 15.

the "thoughtful" member of the group, and an expectant silence followed his presentation. I had decided to be unforthcoming.

"Well," prodded Audrey, "what have you to say?"

What I had to say was violent, so I merely said that I didn't find much food for thought in what I had heard.

"Food for thought!" said Audrey. "You're always thinking, not feeling. You make a god of the mind!"

I should have stopped at this point and left the evening in their hands. But I've never been able to stop, whatever my resolutions.

Late in the evening, when the group had gone, Audrey's dogmatic self had softened to her most contradictory and endearing personality.

"I'm disappointed," she said, "naturally. My friends did less than justice to the Oxford Group." And then she laughed outright, almost as if in confederation. "But I must admit — grudgingly — that I had to admire you."

Kaye telephoned the next morning. "How did it go?"

I gave her a résumé. "And it appears that I make a god of the mind."

"What on earth does she think she knows about the mind. I hope you've had enough now. Why don't you go home?"

"Not at all," I said. "My goal, as always, is to be charmed."

"Well, it's an illness like any other. Good luck."

Ill or not, I couldn't give up the struggle. "Why not have a debate?" I asked Audrey, "— a real discussion, above the level of your backward friends in the Oxford Group? Kaye will come and talk for my side, and you must choose someone for your side. We might be able, for once, to talk like adults."

She agreed that this was a good idea. "But of course I shall win," she added. "People have often put me in this position before, and I have always won them over." By which she meant that emotional conviction is unassailable.

With a resigned exasperation Kaye agreed to cooperate in the "farce," and to bring with her a mutual friend, Eleanor, who could always be counted on to exclaim at the proper moments, "I consider such ideas grim."

For her side Audrey asked a young friend, "Jo-Jo," who (under her personal magnetism) had become a fanatical Christian. I knew the hopelessness of such an encounter, but what good does it do to *know* something when you *believe* in the power of ideas?

The debate began with animation, Audrey and her young disciple convinced that their eloquence would easily crush three superficial opponents.

As it turned out, no eloquence appeared. Eleanor remarked that she had never taken part in a more grisly conversation, that there was no use in going on with it. Kaye finally withdrew into a disgusted silence. Our opponents regarded us without Christian love.

Thus ended the dire evening, to the obvious dismay of Audrey, who, as she explained to me afterward, had for the first time in her life been unable to bring people to her cause.

Despite my frustration and outrage, I was touched by the impersonality with which Audrey said, later that night, "I do understand *something* of what you were trying to say — but what am I to do with someone who is so far from me in thought, yet so near in feeling?"

— 6 —

My three weeks in London were torn between love and the mind.

One day, with the heavy stupidity of youth, I began a dialogue which I hoped would relieve our tension. "You've never said 'radiant of heart' again."

"I can't, I can't," she said. "You've spoiled it all."

"But why?"

"All this talk about lesbianism. How I hate it! That is the barrier between us."

"You don't imagine that I'm among the professional lesbians, do you? I find them as distasteful as you do."

"No, of course not," she said. "But in France everyone talks of these things so openly. We don't do that in England."

"I know you don't. In England everything is accepted if it's well hidden. That makes it right?"

I expected no logic from her. She merely answered, "I may be capable of sinning, but not of calling it right."

"Well, I'm not," I said, "and that, to me, is the barrier between us."

One night, encouraged by some special sense of unspoken love in her manner, I felt that she was going to kiss me goodnight. As I bent toward her I was startled by her reaction. Without moving, simply by looking at me, I felt that she had enveloped me in a cloud of blackness. She herself, the chair in which she sat, the room, my own being . . . I was astounded.

I told Kaye about it the next day. "Interesting," she said. "You really mean blackness?"

"I had an impression of coal-black. I've never been so shocked. It was like being enveloped in evil."

"You probably were," she laughed. "Why on earth do you enjoy this game of cat and mouse? You know that's all there is to it."

"Oh," I said, "I love being a mouse. I've never been one before. And besides, I like a degree of *la belle dame sans merci* in the situation. Love — 'love' — as I've known it has always been so ... call it 'domestic.' No resistance, no opposition, no challenge. It begins, and then it finishes, by a natural law; but one can never be free of it when it finishes because 'the other' is hurt. I want 'love' to follow its natural cycle and then die its natural death, leaving you with memories that will never be duplicated."

"Depends on what kind of love you're talking about."

"Oh you know very well what I'm talking about. Romantic love — the kind that most men seek and wish women knew about; the kind women long for and rarely know how to kindle or to keep alight. It's the stab in the solar plexus, rather than the stab in the heart. The heart stab comes from the deepest love you can know, when you can give a total admiration — like my love for Claire. The other kind is based on charm. You can say that charm is merely animal magnetism if you want to. I don't. Many people have charm, but how many know how to use it (consciously) to create the madness of love? Audrey happens to be the only person I've known who has this power as her *raison d'être*. Love from her would be entirely wonderful. She knows this about herself. She might even 'sin' if she found someone 'worthy' of her."

"You'll never convince her you're worthy if you go on acting as you do. Can't you be clever enough to conceal your brain? Then maybe you can win. Let her believe she's converted you."

"I won't do it."

Kaye walked about the room — bored, impatient, tender, helpless. "Then you may as well give up. It's impossible to influence people by arguing with them. Especially her, with her brand of religion."

"Yes, I know. So I must be satisfied with the game of love as an exciting contest, full of mutual challenge and insult?"

"Well, you'd better equip yourself to play it," Kaye said, and it was my turn to laugh.

A year before, at Christmas, I had sent Audrey a little crèche from Oberammergau — one of those small masterpieces that the Germans and Austrians make with religious love.

"You remember the little crèche?" she asked one day. "I have the sweetest story about it."

It was the story of a poor lonely young creature who had adopted a baby. Her life was re-made; no one had ever loved a baby so much. But one day the Adoption Society discovered that the happy "mother" had once attended a lecture by Bertrand Russell. This frightening news so shocked them that they berated her for days about the sin of listening to Russell. Then they took the baby away from her. She fell ill with grief. The Society kept her in suspense for three months while they debated to what extent the Russell influence made her dangerous to the baby.

"I thought she had suffered enough," Audrey said, "so I persuaded the Society to give the baby back. Before she was told of the decision I went to see her. She was in bed, poor child; she looked *so* ill. I had taken the little crèche with me, and I smiled at her and said, 'This little gift will bring you comfort.' She was *so* grateful. And then, just before leaving, I told her that the baby was being given back to her."

"What a ghastly story!" I said.

We glared at each other like mortal enemies. "What on earth do you mean?"

"You think a smile of yours, and a toy, should make up for those months of anguish?"

"But Bertrand Russell! . . ."

"He's an honest atheist. You can't read him without wishing he had gone further in his 'scientific' research. He might have founded a religion."

* * * * *

78

I decided to make a conscious effort to save the situation before it was too late. The effort succeeded and, as if I had worked a miracle, the observer in me watched Audrey re-assume her happy authority. I was far from happy, and I sat up late to formulate my rebellion in notes which I could take back to Claire:

Result: enchantment recaptured. All the currents on again. A delight — especially when there's confusion as to which is the mouse. But my real reaction: outrage and disgust. Impression of dealing with a monster. Not because of the leading-on and the thwarting (I delight in this), but because of her unawareness of any miracles except physical ones. No mental curiosity about how the charm was recaptured; no consciousness of my effort; satisfaction with the result as if it had depended only on her restored physical dominance; complacency of the organism whose physical seduction was again established and which has no further needs. I had an impression of sloth. An outrage to the mind and spirit. Horrible to watch someone assuming superior "spiritual" behavior when she is rejecting the essence of spirit. And this is the human being who would convert me to "the things of the spirit"! The evil insides of people! — their fundamental immorality, which makes them produce codes of morality. Through the whole experience I had an important revelation of the *why* of her fanaticism. She feels there is some evil in her which she hates and fears; but she has never discovered what it is — just thinks it must be sex. She would root out this evil — she would root it out of all humanity. Therefore the sadistic severity of her code: the whipping-post for lovers.

Everyone found the disparity between my emotions and my criticism hard to understand. To me such a hiatus wasn't astonishing. I tried and tried to explain myself. "I'm not in love with Audrey as a human entity, I'm in love with her as a type. Even if she weren't beautiful, she would still possess her intrinsic seduction. It's not that of the experienced 'charmer,' it's the seduction of an inborn inaccessibility. With such a type you sometimes feel between you so deep a bond of love that it's almost unbelievable; at other times you doubt that you are loved at all. But being loved isn't what matters most to me; *to love* is what matters. Most women are personal, I'm not; most women only want to be assured that they are loved. Nothing holds less promise of seduction. Inaccessibility responds only to love as an art — you have to find the key to it."

"You're certainly not finding it," Kaye said.

"I know I'm not, but I may. At least I know that inaccessibility demands the Art approach. This is as difficult, as mysterious, in life as in literature. And the human Art instrument, like Audrey, is rare — in fact, almost non-existent. I pay my tribute to Art in life as in literature. If I'm a judge of the latter, why not of the former? I can go on trying to create what I most want and most believe in."

"All you'd better believe in is that only one attitude can soften Audrey, and that is admiration for her sainthood."

"Of course, of course. But I can *refuse* to believe it. I can keep on trying to gain her admiration for my convictions."

"Poor little thing!" Kaye said. "But God bless."

On another day of conflict Audrey asked, "Do you think I'm a hypocrite? I know I'm confused — feeling as I do, but realizing that only through self-denial . . ."

"No," I said, "not a hypocrite — you really believe the foolish things you say. Not hypocritical, only neurotic."

She laughed unwillingly. "How *can* you say such things to me?"

"Easily," I said. "Anyone who has decided to live by damming up her physical and emotional energies has poisoned her psyche. *That* is neuroticism."

* * * * *

"What am I to *do* about you?" she asked one day. "How am I to have you in my life?"

"You're to let me be madly in love with you," I said. "No one will know."

"But *we* would know," she said. "You are preposterous."

"No, not I. *You're* preposterous — thinking about the public. The public is an 'unconscious monster,' as Kaye says. Why consider it?"

So she sought out Kaye and repeated her distressed question. "What *am* I to do about her?"

"Regard her as a hybrid — an offshoot, a sport. Why concern yourself so about it? She loves you. You love her?"

"Oh I do, I do . . . but . . ."

"It's of no importance anyhow," Kaye said. "All this emotionalized in-loveness is mankind's most unbecoming state."

I knew that I must leave soon, that the situation would only go from bad to worse if I kept on arguing. So one night I said, "I shall go home now. That's the only perfect thing to do."

"*You* are perfect," she said. "I feel that you are. It's only your ideas that come between us."

She saw me off at Victoria Station. "Oh dear," she said on the platform, "I've forgotten to get you any magazines."

"I don't want any. I shall look out the window."

"And what will you think of?"

"Of what a paradise this world would be if everyone had the right ideas."

"Darling, darling," she said, as the train pulled out.

And my last sight of her was of the lovely face with a mist crossing it, as the indescribable voice said "Goodbye."

— 7 —

To breathe again the free air of France, to recount my London fiasco to Claire, to treasure her comments as one treasures the rewards of Art, to realize that such communication is the bread of life, to be valued as highly as love itself — all this brought me peace.

In the early winter twilight, after the magic hour which the French call *"l'heure bleu,"* when the curtains had been drawn and the candelabra lighted in the old château, when the *valet de chambre* had brought our vermouth-cassis and the fire glowed and silence fell all around us, we talked and talked of love. I read Stendhal's *De l'Amour,* with its science of "crystallization," and Fromentin's *Dominique* and Constant's *Adolphe* — always identifying with the emotions of the hero, never able to share those of the heroine. "That is the interesting thing," Claire said. "It's so authentic in you. Oh, the egoism of human beings — thinking they can tamper with the laws of nature as if they had made them!"

Of course it was still too soon for me to profit fully by Claire's understanding of the psychology of romantic love . . . How can you, when young, realize that romantic love is not so much the longing for fulfillment as for "the prolongation of a madness; not consummation so much as the continuance of a delirium which will be forever renewed"? Its only requisite is the polarity that induces the swoon. Both "normal" and so-called "abnormal" romantic love follow the same laws — which is why romantic lovers should live always in meetings and partings, never in a continuity. There must be "anguish," and there must be "obstruction." But though I still lacked this knowledge, I was imbued with its intimations; and Audrey, being of the same nature and endowed, besides, with the need of attracting rather than of succumbing to love, found in the obstruction of "religion" the perfect background for her relinquishments. It was all as unconscious as Victorian fiction, with its enticements and reluctancies; and it all belonged to the myth that romantic love is the tenderest of passions, when in reality it is the blindest of self-delusions.

Ignoring these realities, I planned my winter. I would write letters to Audrey that would be irresistible in their reasoning. I would make her understand the kind of person I really was, so different from her judgment of me. I would use art and science to convince her of the naturalness of "the love that dares not speak its name." I would be so eloquent that she would come to understand what Kaye once defined as "love that seeks a completion in scarcely definable psychic contacts never intimated or sought by that blind reproductive force called love." Once again, for the millionth time, my only resource in a struggle against the unconscious monster would lie in the words I would write on a piece of paper.

Finally there came a letter from London which began: "Thinking, thinking, thinking what to do" . . . It went on:

Do you see, even through a glass darkly, my point of view?

I have been convinced of the sin which has created the barrier between us. In my very soul I know its destroying power. I know too its subtlety . . . the rapture and beauty it wears as it masquerades before those whose natures demand more beauty than is usually offered in a more wholesome if commonplace relationship. The heart searches for satisfaction — it turns to what seems to offer it.

Have I been unjust to you in any sense? Would it have been more fair to you had I denied — completely denied — your love for whatever you found possible to love in me? I know that love goeth where it listeth, and if it was genuine love for another in you, then to crush it or bruise it is an unthinkable solution. But you must see the effect the barrier has on my love for you. It blinds my eyes, deafens my ears, tortures my mind and makes my heart insensate to the rapture inherent in all you offer.

"Oh," I groaned — "a 'more wholesome if commonplace relationship'! Why not 'wholesome and *non*-commonplace'? How can people be so confused and unseeing?"

I went to my typewriter and, as when I was very young, wrote through the days and nights . . . pompous letters, but at least not lacking in intensity:

Not thinking at all. Suggestions for thought: You have built a moral code which you believe to be unassailable. You built it solely in relation to that part of humanity that is irresponsible. Don't you know any responsible people?

The fact that you venerate man-made laws in respect of the most important human experiences means that you have cut yourself off from greater experiences — for instance, the experience that at a certain level of development one isn't capable of love that is not in all senses elevating.

Everyone knows the harm that organized religion has done in the world. To me there is something unholy in such religion. You have accepted it as the root of your morality. It has become a ferocious, melodramatic *idée fixe*, an obsession.

You say you don't want "dregs." What makes you think you would have them if you don't want them?

Our positions, in respect of love, are identical. You "couldn't enter into a love relation" because you would feel it to be evil. I couldn't enter into such a relation with anyone who felt it to be evil. I wouldn't know what to do, say, think, feel. So references to Satan and temptation are slightly silly.

Therefore I am not a lost sheep pursued by all the hounds of heaven. You speak of possible injustice. There is no injustice toward me except the demand that I accept what I consider a primary, even a malignant, morality. I cannot. It is unjust to make my relation to you hang in the balance of such an acceptance.

I awaited an answer. None came. And then, on a soft November day, the postman brought me a letter in the fabulous handwriting. It was very thick and even before opening it I had a sense of foreboding. This was increased as I saw a second envelope on which was written: "To be read only when you are alone."

The letter was a "renouncement." After a page of Biblical quotations, it stated that she had decided — and the decision was irrevocable — that we must not see each other again. "Can I bear it? I must, and you must too." She was saying goodbye forever because of my ideas. "*My* hope has been that human attraction would lead you to the knowledge of the Living Spirit of Christ. *Your* hope rested in dazzling me into forgetfulness — a perfectly natural hope; but you will remember I told you long ago it would be an unbearable forgetfulness." The rest was in her harshest style: "To me sin corrodes. I am convinced that lesbianism is a vice so soul-destroying to the character that unless one can combat it one should in no wise help or countenance it" . . .

In my first numbness I believed that, at last, outrage would force me to silence. How far I was from measuring the tenacity of my nature, and to what lengths I would go, later, in its determination to convince!

"All this is shameful," Claire said. "I shall write to her myself, and at once."

I have been so distressed, so revolted, by your action that I cannot resist telling you why.

Of the thousands of people I have known in my life, Margaret is the one I should call "pure."

When purity exists in the atmosphere of a human being he ignores it, as do almost all those around him.

One thinks only that such a person has in him something incorruptible and *aéré** which surprises.

I do not understand how you dare usurp the rôle of God in judging that you have the right to change something in such a being.

Anyone who understands the element of the divine which human love contains could never have acted as you have. Even without love for Margaret, a "serious" and "charitable" life would have prevented you from acting toward anyone as you have toward her.

Forgive my frankness. It is dictated by a conviction as strong as it is desolate.

And then, from London, came a letter from Kaye, to whom I had sent a copy of Audrey's letter and my project of a reply:

Really shocked for a time over her letter. So unfitting. Question of deep importance, it seems to me.

Don't send your letter. It won't do a bit of good. No mind there to receive ideas. She doesn't want ideas. She wants you — to eat you alive.

Too adolescent to keep on crusading. All of your arguments belong to one's early twenties, none of them should be in an adult relation. In your letter you disclose your wounds, in a sense remove your mask. Not to be done — dangerous — especially with a woman so cruelly armed with the weapon of her brand of religion. Once behind your mask she will torture you — even more. Torturing is her *métier*. She is a fanatic — religious, sex (same thing really). Fanatics are dangerous — every kind of crime justified, if not actually a "good work."

She has a "belief" — a way of life — that she has "chosen" to follow. If playing with you seems "disobedience" to all this, certainly turning her back on

*Ethereal.

you and taking again a positive attitude toward her belief is an active gesture. It is difficult to wade through all her terms and phrases — so meaningless and hackneyed in her mouth — so mechanical — but when one has swept and dusted and aired one's mind after reading her letter, she is talking about something that means something to her — if no more than a velvet glove over brass knuckles. Well, she has resworn allegiance to this velvet glove. She needs it more than she needs your love and flattery.

See her as she is. Be rid of your illusion about the woman, strip off the unreality. See clearly how she has eaten up your brain and wasted your emotions by being the impetus for endless trains and chains of devitalizing associations (constant drain of energy). If your common sense doesn't tell you that you are simply the victim of a technique that has been used by her on so many young and older women before you — a technique that rejects you and at the same time keeps you writhing... Common sense and a wish to be just to yourself should be enough. But I know that self-intoxication is more deadly than any other form.

"Wonderful letter," I wrote to Kaye, "and probably all true. Except for one statement. You ought to know that I have no illusions about her. I simply want to convince her. Must I die without having this experience of love — this perfection? As they say, one would give one's immortal soul (almost). And then, just imagine that perhaps she loves me a little... This is probably my only illusion. Besides, I'm talking about what *I* want — not what you or others want."

And of course, though I knew it would do no good, I couldn't resist sending my letter.

Our separation is not sin, but two views of sin. Our real separation: two views of "God."

Your decision: a solution for you, imposed upon me. Your solution: "destruction" of a "loved" person in the hope of destroying her loathed ideas.

Has it never occurred to you that ideas cannot be destroyed?

Has it never occurred to you that my life of ideas exists quite apart from your presence or absence, quite apart from my love?

. . . that it exists as definitely as your own?

. . . that it exists more strongly, since I am more attentive to ideas and therefore closer to suffering?

. . . that you have a right to demand whatever conduct you want of people in relation to yourself, but no right to tamper with their ideas?

But this is the history of the world. Self-knowledge — an effort at self-discovery — is necessary to elevate world-history.

You say that "my heart is yearning for something that life all around me fails to offer." True. The life all around me offers me *everything* except the special emotion I have felt for you. I have tried to give this emotion a form, a harmony.

You may feel separated from a "loved" person because you disagree with her. You do not "kill" a loved person because you disagree with her. Love has other resources. Love has the infinite resources of infinite solutions.

I find your letter deeply shocking. I do not accept it. It is not *à-propos*.

I expected, and received, no answer.

But a few days later a small package arrived from London. It was addressed not in her own, but in her maid's, handwriting. In it there was a bottle — an empty bottle — of her perfume.

— 8 —

I could do no more; or at least I hoped that I would do no more, and for four months I held to this resolve. But all that I accomplished during those months was what romantics always arrange for their survival: I loved my suffering without knowing that I was loving it, and made efforts to dominate it that amounted only to the familiar prayer that it would continue rather than that I should find myself out of love.

We stayed on in the château through November. The dragging melancholy days, the brooding old château, all nature seemed to intensify my torment as I walked or drove through the country-side, blinded by pain.

One late afternoon as I drove through the village, an old peasant standing in her doorway waved to me. I was so absorbed in anguish that I forgot to wave back. When I reached the château gates I remembered, and turned the car around and went back past her house and stopped and said, *"Bon soir, madame, comment allez-vous?"* No one must be allowed to suffer disappointment; no one must be allowed to suffer at all if it can be prevented: the slightest hurt must be rectified as soon as possible. I was more fortunate than other people, I had Claire for my protection and consolation. She refused to take my dilemma lightly, to dismiss my delayed adolescence as beneath the consideration of an adult; she spent hours of her time in efforts to lessen my sorrow. How could I ever be grateful enough? And Kaye sent letters from London that taunted me to a revision of my life. Nevertheless I looked upon myself as a victim of unrequited love and doubted that I would ever recover.

* * * * *

In February, when the north of France often has days of advanced spring that compare with the Riviera, I went to visit friends in Normandie — *pour changer les idées*. They lived by the sea in an old *manoir* with few modern conveniences — among other lacks, a telephone.

One night after a tempest had been raging for hours through the darkness, something in its wildness broke down all my resolutions of silence. "I must telephone to London," I thought; "if I don't I shan't be able to go on living."

I drove violently through the storm, racing the twenty *kilomètres* to Le Havre where I would find a telephone in the Hotel Frascatti, in whose bar she and I had so often sat drinking American cocktails and watching the *transatlantiques* come in from New York. Today only the shell of it remains, after the bombings of war.

It was nearly midnight when I put in my call to London in the little enclosed cabin. There was almost no delay. As I said "Hello" a voice spoke in the darkness of the night. It said, "I love you more than anything in the world."

I spoke the beloved name, I heard my own name coming to me in the beloved voice, over hundreds of miles of wire.

"But how did you know? —"

"The operator said France was calling — could it be anyone but you?"

As if neither time nor space had ever separated us, as if the music of her voice had never been withheld from me, she continued to send it to me across the miles. "I've just been to a concert of Bach. I wanted to put the program in an envelope and send it to you. But I threw it away — I knew I mustn't..."

And I knew that I mustn't — so I spoke no words of love; indeed they would have been superfluous. All was known, all was understood — and all was to be thrown away. But I was thinking how grateful I would always be for this miracle of night words. "If you could only see the Light," the voice was saying ... But I had already heard words that were "light" for me — I was loved "more than anything in the world." True? An illusion? Did it matter? I was again enfolded. Love is to the lover. I had a new secret exultation. This was really all I needed to live on. I could again take up my secret life, find new courage, nourish new hope, and believe — as Claire said — in the deposits of Time.

The End

— 1 —

It was six years before I saw her again.

Those years are part of a long and quite other story. They began with an enormous effort, a determination to be "just to myself," as Kaye had urged. I had only to discover the exact meaning of her phrase.

And before too long a time had passed I came to know that most curious phenomenon of romantic love: freedom from it. Once it has been put aside, there comes at last that moment of pause when the heart rests, as after illness, and then comes back to life in a new world — the old familiar world of thought and action. It is as if you had been looking at a picture upside down, and had only to turn it right side up again. Earth and sky reappear, in their proper positions; a sunset exists again for its own sake; a park in the mists of evening exists again as a scene of summer, not merely as "the memory of a handclasp beneath tall trees at night."

Just as — after the death of someone you have deeply loved — sun, moon and stars reshine for you as the great objects of attention, so the death of romantic love frees you again for the greater meaning and mystery behind the visible physical world.

In this new freedom I entered a cycle of abundant, persevering years. And then, after six of them had passed, and as spring came on again once more, I succumbed again to that hunger for a re-creation of my personal life, a self-induced, not-to-be-resisted, re-entry into a state of romance.

I made this decision on a day when primroses were blooming in the woods, and the cuckoo singing in his tree, as

Claire and I walked through the forest, attentive to all the old-new forces coming to life around us.

"I shall try to see her again," I said. "I feel it's the time. Something wonderful must be made to happen. I shall write to her."

"Why not?" Claire said. "You may be able to make her understand at last. You're more mature, and she may have changed in the years."

"Optimist! You know Christian martyrs don't change."

I remember nothing of my letter except one sentence: "Some emotions are permanent, like the one I felt on first seeing you."

I awaited her answer, never doubting that it would be perfect. As Claire had said, "She has two qualities at their height — her charm and the perfection of her responses."

The response came, and it was all I would have asked:

"What rapture to see your handwriting again, among the letters that came up on my breakfast tray. I opened yours last since it was first in importance to me."

"Ah, the rites of spring!" I cried. I was filled with such uncontainable joy that I reminded myself of Stendhal in those letters in which he says he is never indiscreet enough to speak of his love, yet in the next breath writes of it with such exultation that one is thankful the letter has been preserved. I had always loved his saying "I am so full of life that I dare not bend over for fear my cup will overflow." I thought too of Gide's words: "I still have in me an enormous sum of joy that I have found no way of expending." Of joy, I echoed, and of love. And now I would create for myself an experience which was far more likely than an unconscious one to make possible that expending. I wanted the world to reel again; I wanted, again, to turn the picture of heaven and earth upside-down.

By return post I asked her if she wouldn't like to come to France to see the spring. And she answered that nothing would give her greater pleasure . . . and not merely to see the spring.

* * * * *

This time, no matter what happened, I would make none of my fatal mistakes. I would try to match her standards of saying everything in words that said nothing. It was an art that intrigued me, and one I had never practiced.

Is the spring the same everywhere, as I have heard? I have always found the French spring unique. There are really three springs. The first is violets and primroses, which appear as early as February; then almond trees and apple blossoms; then chestnut trees and lilacs. Yes, spring is the same everywhere. Perhaps the difference is that in France you have time to perceive it; and if you live even a few *kilomètres* from Paris, you will sleep and waken to nightingales.

The forest-château was surrounded by the green delight of ascending life. Through all the hours of bright mornings, long twilights and nights under the moon we listened to music.

"Bach," said Audrey, "is the Bible; Beethoven is Shakespeare."

"Chopin," I said — "love and death."

"Even *la musique bon-marché,*"* Claire said, "cannot be rejected, since it springs from life itself."

Only chamber music was barred. Claire and I almost never wanted it. She said, "It sometimes makes my solar plexus so nervous that I've had to leave a concert-hall."

In every measure of music and note of nightingale there resounded for me the triumphant or agonizing history of love in the world, and the realization that because of Audrey Leigh there could exist no recorded love in music or literature to which I would ever feel myself a stranger.

Audrey herself seemed to have put aside, if only for the moment, her self-imposed personality. She talked no more of religion, she appeared to identify herself with my rhapsodic existence. Nevertheless I let the days go by without speaking of love, and the more I avoided speaking of it the more ways she found of luring me on to do so.

We had come back from Paris and had gone into the

---

*Popular music.

rotonde where tea was laid. Claire had not yet come down, and we went on talking as we waited for her.

"I wonder what your ideas of love *really* are," Audrey said. "I can't conceive of giving oneself to a love relationship without being sure it would last. If it didn't, one would be jealous beyond all measure, and then one would despise oneself."

"That's possession, not love," I said. "Why be possessive?"

"One is jealous, that's why. And there's nothing one can do about it."

"Do you enjoy always being wrong?" I asked. "There's nothing disastrous about jealousy, and there's a great deal you can do about it. You don't have to *act* jealous."

"I know what I'm talking about," she said, reverting as usual to her own theme. "Love dies." And then, to my surprise, and as if she were unaware of the revelation I would find in her next words, she went on. "You would tire, change, care for someone else. I will not give myself to tragedy."

"But that's life, Audrey."

Then I realized what I should have said — the kind of thing one is supposed to say at such times, the kind of lie all men tell to all women instead of feeling free to be honest. I couldn't do it. "Love *does* die. But if people knew how to treat it — as I know you would — it might live on."

As she continued to contradict me I saw Claire coming down the stairs. "Do hurry," I called. "Come and tell our benighted guest how wrong she is about everything."

"And you're sure you're right?" Claire said, with a tact I felt to be superfluous.

"I'm sure *you* are," I said. She was writing a book which I felt everyone should be forced to read. "Those pages you showed me the other day — please, please read them now."

I rushed upstairs to find the manuscript, and when I came down my friend and my enemy were smiling at each other like two confederates. I rejoiced at what was to come.

Claire began to read, in her exquisite French, and I watched Audrey's face as she gave her attention to inspired words which I knew were going to surprise and shock her:

Jealousy? Its manifestations are absurd and insane, but not without a certain grandeur. I pity people who have not known it. It has taught me much.

And passion? We are told to be tolerant of it — what presumption! We are asked to pity, to try to understand. The beauty of passion is there is nothing to understand, only something to look at and envy. I would be in despair if I had to die without having known this cyclone. The magnificence of passion is that no human force can stop it.

Passion, when it has measure, is admirable. These two words — passion and measure — seem a contradiction? Nevertheless it is from this antithesis that all great things are made. Directed passion is a great orchestral symphony — this is the substance from which a perfect thought of Pascal is molded, as well as every other manifestation of genius. It is in creative genius that the grandeur of passion is seen; in life most human beings are too frail to cope with it — this gift of flames from which they should arise, purified, generally leaves them diminished. This fiery gift is greater than the human being who carries it, and whatever is greater than man must be regarded objectively in order not to shrink the materials Nature has given him.

As I had expected, there was no uplifted response in the face I watched.

"Beautiful words," she said, "but I'm afraid they have no reality for me. I know the slavery of love. It grows by what it feeds on. You want it all the time."

"Why?" Claire asked. "You don't want music all the time. It would lose its power."

She and I had merely lost an argument.

On another day of conflict I parried a clash with a cleverness that astonished me afterward. Encouraged by my lack of belligerence, Audrey reverted to the old discussion. "The day will come," she said, "when you will see the light as I see it. What a day of rejoicing that will be for me!"

"Rejoicing? You have a faith and I have a faith. That should be a matter of mutual rejoicing."

She gave me a glance of reluctant appreciation and said, *"Touchée."*

— 2 —

Her visit was nearing its end, and one late afternoon we walked through the winding paths of the forest and farther on into the spring fields.

I said, "In August these fields will be filled with pink clover, and there'll be an enormous pink moon."

"And I won't be here," she said, linking her arm in mine. Her topaz ring and her electric fingers rested on my hand. "I really can't bear to go."

"Then don't," I said, keeping my voice unmoved.

We sat down on the terrace of a roadside café at the end of the village and spent an hour, as one can always do in France, in the freedom and protection of anonymity.

She sat in silence. Her eyes roamed over the empty tables, examined the *patronne* who brought our drinks, gazed out over the fields, looked at everything but me. Then, leaning her face on her hand, and looking carefully at the table, she said, "I have been wondering" — she hesitated — "whether you still . . ."

"Oh, dearest Audrey, I shall always feel this way. Is there any power on earth strong enough to turn me from loving Chopin? It's the same kind of love."

"Then you must rest in the absolute knowledge that there is only love in my heart too. I must say it to you, and you will know it." She raised her head and looked at me. Shall I ever forget her eyes?

The sun was setting as we started back across the fields. We walked silently as if words, having been used at last for their purpose — that of conveying meaning — left nothing more to be said.

As we approached the château a servant stood at the top of a flight of steps, ringing the dressing-gong for dinner. Before the gates Audrey walked more slowly, as if she were weighing important words. Then she stopped and said in a low voice, barely audible above the ringing of the bell, "I can accept a state of love, not an act of love."

And I said, "But what do you think I'm always talking about? A state of love is what I love."

During the last days of her visit I moved in a trance of all the ecstacies. I no longer needed food or sleep. I was no longer a victim of unrequited love, but only of what Yeats called "that monstrous thing, *returned* yet unrequited love." It wasn't, to me, a monstrous position. It was even, I felt, an enviable one, since I saw no one else who was as much in love as I was.

Yet how could I be fully happy? The issue between us was unresolved, which left my mind seething. And besides, love should move toward its natural evolution . . . which would be for me, as for all lovers, "that moment of all moments upon earth."

What was monstrous was the idea of original sin — the root of her religion. Why hadn't I the power to combat this established and malevolent conception? My distress wasn't merely personal. What troubled me was the fact that even the world's "great minds" have accepted original sin as the basis of their morality. How many more years before people evolve to a higher level of consciousness? As many as are demanded for the great slow movements of science — almost two thousand years for the discovery of the atom bomb. How many more before humanity discovers a new consideration of the soul of man?

Ah! to convince with my convictions! How could I be so sure of being right? — I, one small individual, be so sure of my ground? How does one become *sure* of anything? By being shown a higher concept, which shows the lower one to have been but a step.

Since I could never convince her, why go on trying? One is convincing only to those on the same level of experience; one is convincing only when it isn't necessary to convince. I had done my best to present a standard of love. That it had met with profanation had robbed years of my life of . . . what? "Of dignity,"

Kaye would say. I don't say or think such things. Perhaps I don't know what dignity is, or, if I do, it isn't something on which I place a highest value. I prefer madness.

As for the madness of love — I didn't feel that I had been cheated. I knew that I would never again find in anyone the exact combination of those ingredients my nature demands for the ultimate spell of love — a rite rather than a function. (And I never have.) Therefore I was grateful to have found it.

As for the mind's madness . . . perhaps without its exigencies I might long since have attained this "sharper" love. No, no — all perfect things, for me, must have the mind's support; and I didn't yet know that it is not the mind which has power over prejudice and pain.

— 3 —

*W*e were to drive to Dieppe, to the channel ferry for Newhaven. We would drive slowly, savoring the countryside, and stop for a night in one of those inns on the Seine, at Le Petit Andely, where you dine beside the river and listen to the movement of olive-green water against the embankment, and to the slow boats that pass, with their red and green lights, so close to your table that you could almost reach out and touch them.

The visit had ended on a flawless note, untroubled by tensions or antagonisms.

"I'm learning how to act," I said to Claire the night before we left. "And now I don't have to learn what will follow, since I know it so by heart: all the days to come when that face, that presence, are as needed as electricity, when every hour holds the hope of a letter. All the old 'enslaving factors' of which I'm such a willing victim."

"*Quand même, tout cela a une certaine grandeur,*"* Claire said.

"And it's strange," I said, "but I begin to feel something else. I've a dim impression that I've been colossally stupid. I don't know just what I mean, but it's like a new idea in my brain."

When we reached the inn on the river, we found it filled with lilacs, and our table on the terrace held a great vase of them, as if by command. Two, three hours went by as we dined and boats drifted up and down the river, filling the air

---

*Even so, all that has a certain grandeur. — Ed.

with that putt-putt peculiar to Seine river boats and which, once heard, can never be forgotten.

As darkness fell, the waitress brought candles to our table, and in their flickering light I watched the shadows on Audrey's changing face.

Of all that we talked about, I remember three things she said. One was, "What about the person who has what you call 'personal effulgence' — who has it for many people; do you say she has more to give to 'the one person,' or less?"

"Oh," I said, "more, much more." And she turned on such a powerful current of charm that I could only wonder, blinded, what would be its incandescence if she ever decided to choose me as the one person. She went on talking about love as if she alone in the world knew what it could be, and I knew that I would never forget this night — the silence, the water and lilacs, the soft candle-light, the rising moon, the cadences of an incomparable voice, and the display of all the most potent allurements offered by a connoisseur for my expert appreciation.

We lingered over coffee and she asked, "Shall we put out the candles and have only the moon?"

We sat on for a long time. I was preoccupied with the realization that we were sharing that special communication which is beyond the power of words to bestow. And in the fullness of peace that invaded my heart I heard her say, "I think no one has ever really loved me. It has always been simply a question of attraction."

"But Audrey," I said, with quiet desperation, "I love you."

"Do you?" she said. "Really . . . ?" And for the first time since I had known her I saw sadness in her face.

I had never felt so close to her — to her, the person she really was, separate from her ideas, from all that was distorted in her by a constricting religion. "You must know" — I began; and then rushed on, "Oh I have so many new things to tell you! . . ."

She looked at me as she had in the little roadside café. "Perhaps I feel them," she said. She put her hand across the table and I covered it with mine — that vital hand, so vibrant that even to touch it held a wildness more keen than any other I have known. We sat looking at one another in a slow dream and finally she said, "Perhaps there is no need, now, to *tell* me."

Then she withdrew her hand and rose from the table, turning abruptly from me and walking to the balustrade, where she stood looking out over the water.

"Should you like to walk along the river?" I asked.

But she merely said, "No. Shall we go?"

It was late as we entered our rooms, with their balconies on the river and the moon shining full into their shadowed alcoves, and lilacs everywhere. We said goodnight as if we shouldn't say it, and I went to my room in a daze of loveliness and love.

I undressed quickly and stood for a long time on my balcony, looking at the moon and its image on the water, conscious of the divinity of night; conscious too that it was not a night to be made more divine by the divinity of love. Why? Why? I kept asking, as I had done for so long. but after a moment the flood of new impressions that had been racing through my mind quieted and cleared. Stupid — hadn't I been too stupid, somewhere, in my rationalizations? Why, even, had I rationalized at all — or, if at all, why not all the way? Tonight for the first time in my "love" for Audrey I had felt the stab in the heart that belongs to love. *This* was what she had known was lacking; this was what the sadness in her face had meant? I had talked for years about being in love; I had basked in the love of love, but what had I really felt of Love? I had made a distinction between the love that is based on total admiration and the love that stops short of it. *This* was immaturity, and was I never to advance beyond it? I had been so convinced of the superiority of my ideas! Well, they *were* superior, but was love dependent on ideas? In romantic love (I remembered Kaye saying) the ideas in one's head are of no more importance than the food in one's stomach.

And I had believed that a divergence of faith was fatal. Wasn't this also a blindness of immaturity? No one should try to destroy the faith of another — I had heard this said, but I had never given it a moment's real thought. I had spent my time with Audrey in challenge, defiance, even scorn. Of course if she hadn't attacked *my* faith first perhaps I wouldn't have attacked hers. (Oh, be honest, I thought. Of course I would.)

But the point lay elsewhere. Nothing is superior except that understanding which understands all things. And that is the meaning of "the greatest of these is love"? It alone produces miracles? Not the mind but the heart? And this is part of the "objective love" Douglas talked about, and which, until now, I thought I had understood? How blind I had been for years . . . Oh, oh, I must remember to tell her in the morning. Perhaps she had already felt the change in me. Was this why she had said there was no need to *tell* her now?

And then, did I hear my name called — softly, from the next room? No, it couldn't be — it was only a last hope of my heart. But I heard it again . . . that blurred voice I had loved for so many years. I felt my life stop in my veins. But no, it could only mean another goodnight — "Goodnight, and again and yet again goodnight" . . . I left the balcony and walked slowly toward the voice, without hope or design.

She was holding out her beautiful arms. "I shan't fight it any longer," she said . . . "I love you."

Had I wept with love, with an ecstasy outshining all I had known this love would be? My eyes were clear of tears as I watched hers open in the morning light.

"Audrey, Audrey," I said — "a state of love?"

Her dominant head lay against my cheek. She raised her eyes and looked at me clearly and held my face in her hands as she murmured breathless words I had thought never to hear again.

"I am radiant of heart," she said.

— 4 —

Years and years and years ago . . .

I shan't say that it lasted "forever." It had a deeper time, a time in height and depth. It gave us unbearable partings, unbelievable meetings — a full life-span. It had its ending, but it never came to its end.

She knew the perfect moment to part, as I had always known she would, the parting that cheats life of its repetitions, its reductions, and that belongs to a knowledge outside the possession of nearly all human beings.

She took up her life once more, and I mine. We never discussed religion again. She kept hers, and I kept mine. She had cherished her own too long to change it, but I think she understood something of mine, at last.

And then there were letters that created for us once more a secret bond beneath all the other events of living. Thus all was kept in the regions of the heart's great longings, and withheld from those regions where they have been over-fulfilled. All had belonged to the young, the too-beautiful, the endlessly-renewed.

And years later, as she lay dying in a country far away, she sent me a last letter. The strength of her handwriting had not diminished; it still swept forward like the sails of a ship riding the seas. I have always kept the letter near me, for in it she evoked once again the radiance we had known. Even today that memory has such a poetry and permanence that it moves beside me like a sustaining power.

Lois, Jean and Margaret Anderson, Youngstown, Ohio, 1896.

"This is one of my favorite pictures—at Lake Wawasee, Indiana, when I was about fifteen. I am sitting at the extreme left; then my unconscious crush; then the girl who wished on the stars to be as popular as I was; then Lois; then the boy in love who wept because I had forgotten the roses waltz" (M.C.A.).

Jane Heap, the summer she and Margaret took *The Little Review* to Mill Valley, California, 1916.

Harriet Dean, the summer Margaret and her magazine staff camped beside Lake Michigan, 1915.

Jane Heap as an Irish king in Yeats's *On Baille's Strand* at Chicago's Little Theatre, Fine Arts Building, 1912. (Courtesy of the University of Michigan Library).

"Mart" as Margaret was known in the Chicago days of *The Little Review*. Photograph by Hutchinson.

Secret of Woman Editor's Success— Belief That Nothing Is Commonplace

OWNER OF ULTRA-MODERN MAGAZINE AIMS TO ESTABLISH MEDIUM FOR STRUGGLING WRITERS.

MARGARET ANDERSON

"For every difficulty there is some approach, some victory."

Margaret in New York, before *The Little Review* was confiscated and burned by the U.S. Postal Service.

Jane Heap in New York, photographs by E.O. Hoppé.

LEFT TO RIGHT—EDITH WILLIAMS, LOUISE DAVIDSON,
DE WOLF HOPPER, AND HELEN TILDEN.
[TRIBUNE Photo.]

Louise Davidson (second from left) and her companion, actress
Gladys Helen Tilden (far right) on tour in *The Better Ole*, 1920.

"For Margaret Anderson—a charming friend who embodies the precious miracle of possessing as much heart as beauty! as much beauty as spirit and soul, Affectionately, Georgette Leblanc, New York, May 25, 1921."

Margaret and Georgette at Brookhaven, Long Island, New York, July 1921.

Margaret at Brookhaven.

Georgette at Brookhaven, Margaret's and Jane's summer home.

Georgette and Margaret at their self-styled "art colony" with composer George Antheil, Bernardsville, New Jersey, 1921.

Georgette (right), about to depart on a European concert tour with Margaret (left) as her accompanist. Louise Davidson (center) acted as their manager, May 1923.

Georgette aboard the "S.S. Paris".

"We sailed for France and all Georgette's [sister's] 'palaces'—which she never mentioned" (M.C.A.).

Margaret, embarking for France, 1923.

Margaret, visiting Georgette's sister at the
Château de Tancarville, 1923.

L'INHUMAINE

Histoire féérique vue par MARCEL L'HERBIER

Interprétée par :

GEORGETTE LEBLANC
JAQUE = CATELAIN
PHILIPPE HÉRIAT
L. = V. DE MALTE =:= KELLERMAN

Décorée par :

FERNAND LÉGER
MALLET = STEVENS
PIERRE CHAREAU
CL. AUTANT = LARA
ALB. CAVALCANTI

Georgette as "Claire Lescot" in the 1923 L'Herbier film, *L'Inhumaine.*

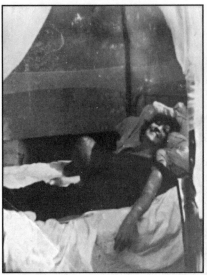

Georgette at Tancarville, 1923.

Georgette on the set of *L'Inhumaine*.

Margaret in her "Annette Kellerman" pose, 1927.

Georgette on the beach at Cannes, 1927.

The Prince von Turn und Taxis invited Georgette to perform *St. Sebastien* for the neighboring aristocracy, Margaret accompanying on the piano, Duino, Italy, 1928.

Margaret at Gardone, Italy, 1925.

The Prince von Turn und Taxis, Georgette and Margaret.

Jane Heap, photographed in Paris
by Berenice Abbott, 1927.

Georgette at the Tancarville Lighthouse, 1928.

Margaret in 1928.

English couturier Elspeth Champcommunal, companion of Jane Heap until Jane's death in 1964.

"This is the day when Gurdjieff, visiting the Lighthouse, disliked Georgette's too-exhuberant greeting. I was in favor that day because I was arranging the tables, the view, the service and all practical matters" (M.C.A.).

The Lighthouse above the Seine, summer home of Georgette, Margaret and Monique Serrure, 1928-1938.

Solita Solano, author of *The Uncertain Feast* (1924) and *This Way Up*, 1927.

Margaret and Solita at the Neuilly Fair, Paris, 1928.

Allen Tanner, Solita and Margaret at the wedding of Elslpeth Champcommunal's daughter, Paris, 1928.

Margaret, photographed by Solita at Le Mesquer, 1928.

Solita Solano, the year she met Margaret,
photographed by Berenice Abbott, Paris, 1927.

Georgette in the *rotonde* of the tumble-down Château de la Muette
in the Forest of St. Germain-en-Laye, 1932.

Gladys Tilden's aunt, Josephine Plows-Day, "Tippy", 1937.

Georgette at St. Pardoux in the Corrèze, August 1940.

Margaret at St. Pardoux, 1940.

G.I. Gurdjieff, philosopher-mystic, the subject of Margaret's 1962 study, *The Unknowable Gurdjieff.*

In the car given her by "Tippy", Margaret, with Monique Serrure and the ailing Georgette, fled the Germans in 1940.

The tiny Chalet Rose, Le Cannet, "our war refuge when we had no other place to go" (M.C.A.).

Margaret carrying in coal at the Chalet Rose, 1940.

Solita and Janet Flanner at Tumble Inn,
Croton-on-Hudson, New York, 1940.

Kathryn Hulme, Solita, Janet Flanner
and Alice Rohrer at Croton-on-Hudson,
1940.

Margaret and Gladys Tilden (standing), with Gladys's companion, Dorothea Huckle
(seated, center) at Les Bastides-sur-Siagne, near Le Cannet, 1941.

Monique at the Chalet Rose, her home throughout the war.

Georgette, a few months before her death in 1941, with Monique at the Chalet Rose.

Margaret, photographed by Solita after her arrival in New York, July 1942.

Elizabeth Jenks Clark (Lib) at the time she met Solita, 1942.

Solita in her A.W.V.S. uniform, New York, 1942. Photograph by Pat Wilkinson.

Margaret, left, and Dorothy Caruso, widow of the tenor, whom she met on shipboard, relaxing at Mt. Kemble, Morristown, New Jersey, July 1942.

Dorothy Caruso and Isabelle Pell, a member of the French Resistance in Auribeau, 1941.

Dorothy Caruso, 1943.

136

Solita and Lib at Mt. Kemble, 1952.

Solita, with their kitten, "Chessie". Photograph by Elizabeth Clark, 1942.

137

Solita Solano (left), Alice Rohrer, Dorothy and Margaret, and Alice's companion, author Kathryn Hulme at Mt. Kemble. Photograph by Elizabeth Clark, 1942.

Alice Roher, Margaret and Solita (seated) and Dorothy and Marylka Patterson (standing), Mt. Kemble. Photograph by Elizabeth Clark, 1946.

Lib (left), Solita and Vera Daumal Page (seated) and
Margaret and Dorothy (standing), Orgeval, 1955.

Dorothy, Noel Murphy and Janet Flanner, Orgeval,
1949.

Margaret with Dorothy
(seated) in the late
'forties.

Margaret, in painter's costume, at *"Les Hiboux"*, Orgeval, 1962.

Solita and Margaret at *"Les Hiboux"*, 1962.

Lib, Solita, her hand bitten by a muskrat, and Daphne Fielding, Orgeval, 1966.

Margaret, age 81, dining at the Hotel Majestic, Cannes, 1967.

Hotel Reine des Prés,
Margaret Anderson's last home, Le
Cannet. Photograph by
Tina Letcher.

Margaret and Lib
at the graves of Georgette and Monique,
Le Cannet, 1966: "I knew what she was
thinking—'Soon I'll be there, too' "
(E.J.C.).

Malou Habets (left),
the "nun" of
Kathryn Hulme's
The Nun's Story,
Solita, Margaret,
and Lib, Le
Cannet, 1966.
Photograph by
Kathryn Hulme.

Margaret, listening to
Moura Lympany at the
Chalet Rose, 1967.

Editor's Postscript

I came across a 1921 photograph recently of my mother aboard a ship bound for France. I think it was my mother, although her head doesn't show — only her three dogs, a wire-haired fox terrier, a Belgian shepherd and a bulldog, and her legs. My mother's Right Bank Paris lasted ten years while she sculpted animals, raised dogs, and was courted by my handsome father, then a student of architecture and frequenter of that cradle of French modernism, Le Boeuf sur le Toit on the rue Boissy d'Anglas.

My mother used her talents well. With her gifted hands, all during the Depression years she crafted stylish leather clothes and, aided by French-speaking seamstresses, started her own business, The Leather Tailor.

My parents' stories of life in Paris took on a new dimension when in 1940 their expatriate friends came to our house, exhausted by their flight from France. I remember one summer afternoon, as we sat in canvas lawn chairs sipping tea in the shade of the soughing pines, the Beekmans and Sophie de Enden anxiously told of friends left behind, of hurriedly buried belongings, of trunks deserted on railway platforms.

Years later a graduate school professor mentioned in passing, while introducing Joyce's *Ulysses* to a class, that it was first serialized in *The Little Review* by Margaret Anderson and Jane Heap, two of THOSE women in Paris in the twenties.

After reading Margaret Anderson's story of a transcendent love for Georgette Leblanc in *The Fiery Fountains*, the perfect antidote to *The Well of Loneliness*, I wrote her a fan letter, care of her publisher. An envelope of great beauty arrived from France, decorated with a stamp of a magnificent Lascaux cave painting. The address, underlined in three colors, was handwritten with great sloping M's. In a perfectly typed letter Margaret Anderson thanked me and went on to say, "I'm working madly on Private Papers and Letters that are to become the MCA Collection." Her next communication was on the back of a dark blue postcard, "Midnight on the Côte d'Azur," saying she was very ill. That October, 1973, she died.

A few months later, in a back issue of *The Ladder*, I read that Gene Damon hoped to find out about the years in Margaret Anderson's life since the death of Dorothy Caruso, her last love. "Perhaps they are recorded . . . perhaps not. We are lucky if someday they will appear" (October/November 1970). In another issue *The Ladder* tantalizingly reported a rumor of an unpublished novel.

Then at a Modern Language Association conference in late 1974 Bertha Harris spoke movingly about rediscovering the Paris lesbians. Quoting from her now-famous essay, she cited *The Autobiography of Alice B. Toklas* as "the book of ancestors": "Our family bloodline, the common identity among us, would always be nothing more, nothing less, than our common need for the word of consequence: will always be my acknowledgment of these women, despite all material difference between us, as my first ancestors. . . ." ("The More Profound Nationality of Their Lesbianism: Lesbian Society in Paris in the 1920's," in *Amazon Expedition*, New York, 1973, pp. 78–79).

Thanks in large measure to notes written by Gene Damon, a.k.a. Barbara Grier, in *The Ladder* and the hint of an unpublished novel, and thanks to a fortuitous impulse, I wrote to a distant cousin, Gertrude Macy (the "Gert" in Paul Monette's *Last Watch of the Night*), a marvelously knowledgeable woman of the arts world in New York and for many years actress Katherine Cornell's general manager, telling her my plan to write a biography of Margaret Anderson and asking how I might reach Janet Flanner. Gertrude Macy replied that my letter happened to be well timed: Margaret Anderson's good friend Mrs. Elizabeth Jenks Clark had just arrived from France for a brief stay in New York.

Gertrude Macy,
Mathilda Hills and
Elizabeth (Lib) Clark,
Snedens Landing,
New York, 1978.

April 1976: Two days after I wrote Mrs. Clark, she telephoned, inviting me to come to New York from Rhode Island and talk about "Margaret." We met at her hotel — she a spirited woman in her sixties with deep-set brown eyes and curly gray hair. Her manners were formal, yet she was completely natural. Dressed in a white woolen jacket with gold buttons, Hermès scarf, pearl earrings, and tailored beige slacks, she seemed to have an innate sense of style, not just in her clothes but in her entire bearing. She suggested lunching at an Italian restaurant on Irving Place, and it was only as we walked slowly around Gramercy Park that she revealed she had been ill, had come to New York Hospital for treatment of osteoporosis.

At lunch Lib — as I came to call her later — asked if I had seen the scrapbooks her great friend Solita Solano had created during her years in Paris with Janet Flanner and donated, along with many letters from Margaret, to the Library of Congress. No, I hadn't even heard of them then. Lib had known Margaret since the war when she herself, in the American Women's Voluntary Service, had met Solita in New York. She told me she had been a sculptor, that she was born in Narragansett, Rhode Island, where her family summered, and that her fish fountain,

145

sculpted in Paris when she knew Gertrude Stein, Alice B. Toklas and Janet Scudder, stood near the Towers in Narragansett.

I was struck by Lib's remarkable gift for articulating a great range of feelings, a gift that as a reticent New Englander I especially admired. Clearly she had a great affection for Margaret, the one person, she said, with whom she could discuss absolutely anything. Evident throughout our conversation

Louise Davidson in her A.W.V.S. uniform, Ridgefield, Connecticut, 1942.

was her devotion to Solita, who had died in France the previous autumn at age eighty-eight. In a deeply expressive voice, colored by warm tones and varied inflections, Lib spoke candidly yet with subtlety, as one accustomed to saying what she meant, but paying the listener the compliment of not spelling it out. She allowed for silence and she connected.

Mid-April, in Washington for a Shakespeare Conference, I went to the Library of Congress to see the scrapbooks. Solita

Solano had meticulously kept records of the years from 1914 on, telling the story of her career as a reporter, publicist and novelist in Boston and New York, of her life in Paris with Janet Flanner at 36 rue Bonaparte, and of their circle of friends, including Margaret. As I opened each scrapbook, still smelling of paper paste, I felt as an archaeologist must on first entering an ancient site. With some surprise I came upon a photograph of Louise Davidson, a woman I remembered from work together in the White Barn Theatre in Westport, Connecticut. Why hadn't I been more curious about the background of this soft-spoken elderly woman, wearing a French beret, who spoke with girlish enthusiasm of Paris in the twenties? Among the letters, one from Janet Flanner to Margaret after publication of *The Fiery Fountains* intrigued me, alluding to an untold chapter in Margaret's life. In it Janet chastised her for focusing only on one aspect of her life and "in one of your characteristic gestures, darling, [stacking] things in the closet or under the carpet" (12/13/1951, Library of Congress).

In New York again in late April I learned that Lib planned to return to France mid-May, sell her house and move to America to be near her son and grandchildren. For now she was eager to get back to Orgeval and Bébé Chou, the cat she and Solita had found as an orphaned kitten in a cabbage patch.

I don't know what made me write offering to accompany Lib back to Orgeval should she like any help on the long journey. I had already made plans for the summer to work at the Folger Shakespeare Library and, later, to join my love, who taught at another New England college. In the middle of a violent thunderstorm, with a brilliant flash of lightning, Lib telephoned, "Yes, come! Do you have your passport? Can you arrange your ticket on Air France from New York on May 28th?" Yes! No, I didn't have my passport, but would get one pronto, and yes, I would call Air France for the ticket.

Two weeks later we flew overnight to Charles de Gaulle where we were met and driven out through the Saint Cloud tunnel, forty kilometers west to Orgeval. It was Pentecôte, the pear blossoms had just fallen, and the traffic was horrendous, the French, as was the custom, making a long holiday — *Il fait le pont.* We drove up the rue Feucherolles from the village to the little enclave of Haut Orgeval, then onto a narrow lane bordered by whitewashed houses with orange-tiled roofs. In the side of a walled incline was a wrought-iron gate with steps behind it. Very stiff from the long journey, Lib stepped out of the car and together we opened the creaking gate. As we climbed six or seven stone steps up beneath a gatehouse, a pale pink stucco house emerged into view, its French windows edged by climbing roses, then a garden, all enclosed by walls. Suddenly a small, long-haired tortoiseshell cat rushed up and stood on Lib's foot, greeting with all her might. "*Oh, Bébé Chou! Tu fais le ron-ron!*," Lib said, bending over loud purrs.

The front door opened into a small well-lit dining room, then to a comfortable salon with a medieval-looking fireplace flu and a huge glass door which swung out on a track into the sunken patio. Solita's etymological dictionaries — her "drugs," she called them — filled a table at the end of the salon alongside a wall of books and records. Photographs of their friends — Margaret in profile, Janet Flanner, Nancy Cunard, Isak Dinesen, and Lib's family, and Bébé Chou, capped by a Christmas crown — decorated two tables. Although out beside the stone steps the gatehouse beckoned, Solita had always preferred to work right at the dining room table. This was also Bébé Chou's dining room. Atop a narrow telephone table, twice daily she was served her fresh-cooked liver. Up a narrow staircase were two rooms. Lib's, as austere as Van Gogh's yellow bedroom, faced both lawn and alley. Solita's room faced the lawn and was furnished with a cherry-red rug, a bedside table and a Chagall print. I was struck by the simplicity of life here. There was little beyond necessities.

The next morning I walked down the rue Feucherolles, past workmen pausing for their morning ritual, not of coffee, but a *coup de rouge,* and crossed the muskrat stream into Orgeval. I stopped at a café opposite the ancient village church, then walked up the hill to Lib's gate. Just beyond her wall, in Mlle. du Torta's garden, lay Bébé Chou, snoozing in the shade of a cabbage leaf.

That afternoon Lib gestured to a wooden trunk at the far end of the salon next to the dictionaries: "Here are Margaret's letters." Here indeed, in packets neatly tied with ribbon. Hundreds of letters passed between Le Cannet and Orgeval between 1956 and 1973. For Margaret, living in isolation at the Chalet Rose after Dorothy's and Monique's deaths and later in a room at the Hotel Reine des Prés, letters were places of meeting, a "*café* on paper," just as *The Little Review* had been a "*salon* in print." She typed messages on the right half of the paper only, inviting Solita and Lib — whom she alone called "Lynn" — to reply directly on *their* left side.

Margaret shared her interests with her friends, sent them manuscripts for comment, inquired about their lives, offered advice and occasionally introduced controversy, especially on Gurdjieff, a topic Solita was reluctant to discuss. At age eighty Margaret became entranced by English pianist Moura Lympany, avidly following her career, even arranging to meet her after a concert in Monte Carlo. True, her world was filled with memories of now-dead loves Jane, Georgette and Dorothy, but her *awareness* centered on the present and visits with Solita and Lib in Orgeval or Le Cannet. Her correspondence kept up the steady "conversation" Margaret had sought since *Little Review* days.

Since November 1975, when Solita died, Lib had lived alone in Orgeval. She had moved there in 1958 to join Solita, then helping Janet Flanner with her *New Yorker* "Letter from Paris." Before buying their house, Lib and Solita had shared a guest house, *Les Bouillons,* on property owned by Janet and Noel Murphy across from the Moulin d'Orgeval. A very frail Janet Flanner arrived from New York during my stay, and Noel invited Lib and me to lunch. Noel was imposing, even a bit frightening, with a habit of saying whatever came to her mind, and Janet Flanner was fun. Even in her dotage she relished talking — in her unique version of an English accent. She delighted in watching the robins get drunk on rotten apples in the garden and teased me, "Aren't you a bit *raffinée* for a professor?" (In those days I wore dresses to luncheon parties.) Hearing that I planned to write about Margaret Anderson, she exclaimed, "Margaret! Mad as a March hare! The most educated person I ever knew, but in a useless way." Yes — and no. There was an undercurrent — Margaret had come between Janet and Solita long ago.

Living with Noel was Libusse Novak, a Czechoslovakian pianist who had accompanied Noel when she sang *lieder* and stayed on to help farm the property. For the summer, to escape Noel's shrieked commands for help with Janet, Libusse had created a refuge for herself in the abandoned pigsty.

Reading letters in Lib's salon, I asked if Margaret had written a novel. Yes, Lib remembered it well. Did the manuscript exist? She thought so, but to find the answer I should meet Michael Currer-Briggs, she said, the English "Gurdjieff person" who arranged the sale of Jane Heap's *Little Review* papers to the University of Wisconsin-Milwaukee. Michael was devoted to the memory of Jane Heap, and consequently to everyone connected to Jane. Just after Margaret Anderson's death in 1973 he had gone to Le Cannet, acting on behalf of her estate, had packed up her papers and taken them to London. Lib telephoned Michael, then working in Paris with Peter Brook on the film of Gurdjieff's autobiographical *Meetings with Remarkable Men,* invited him out to Orgeval, and arrangements were made for my departure for London.

Late into our last evening, while the June twilight lingered, Lib and I sat out on the sunken terrace. *Les hiboux,* after whom her place was named, began softly to whoo-whoo in the short night, and little putt-putts sounded from the fields in the darkness, supposedly frightening hungry creatures from the strawberry plants.

After saying goodbye to Lib at the station in Villennes, I took the train to the Gare St-Lazare and flew to London. Michael's flat was in St. John's Wood, not far from the house Jane and Elspeth Champcommunal had shared in Hamilton Terrace. In his sunny living room, beneath a Tchelitchew portrait of Jane, he set out two handsome leather traveling bookcases, bought, he said, by Dorothy Caruso. The papers, hastily packed, remained

Lib at *Les Hiboux*,
Orgeval, 1976.
Photograph by
Mathilda Hills.

in manila folders, just as Margaret had left them. One by one I opened them: letters, photographs, reminiscences and the manuscript for *Forbidden Fires*. Here were the stories Janet Flanner had accused Margaret of stacking "in the closet."

Here too was a letter from Jeannette Foster, dated June

Mathilda, Orgeval,
1976. Photograph by
Elizabeth Clark.

Lib in Santa
Fe, New
Mexico, 1978.
Photograph by
Mathilda Hills.

Lib, Bébé Chou
and Mathilda,
Kingston, Rhode
Island, 1982.

1960, with her comments on the novel and with the publication history of her own lesbian book, the ground-breaking *Sex Variant Women in Literature* (see Appendix).

That summer of 1976, through letters, I kept up with Lib's progress on the sale of her house. Expecting her return to New York one day in September, I waited for her telephone call. A call came, not from Lib but a friend in Paris. Lib was in the American Hospital at Neuilly. Alone in her house, she had fallen and broken her hip. She would have to undergo surgery. In those moments I realized that I might lose Lib, and that I couldn't endure losing her because I'd fallen in love with her. Looking back, I remembered a stop on our drive to the Cathedral at Chartres when I'd decided against a solitary walk to the fabled Château of Mme. de Maintenon in favor of sitting in the diesel fumes of a roadside café, just to be a few extra minutes with Lib.

Not until November did Lib return to New York, this time bringing Bébé Chou with her. I spent a winter's leave with Lib in New York and Santa Fe, continuing research for a biography of Margaret Anderson, and it was then we planned to make our home together. We shared the same interests, the same sensibilities, the same pleasures in life. The following September Lib and Bébé Chou joined me in my apartment in Kingston, and there we lived until Lib's death, at home, her son and I at her bedside, in March 1989.

The little fish fountain stands guard by the Towers near the entrance to Narragansett Bay, symbolizing for me the idea of

France that first drew me across the ocean with Lib and, finally, drew us together in this place of her birth.

Lib in front of her fish fountain, Narragansett, Rhode Island, 1983. Photograph by Mathilda Hills.

Appendix

Margaret Anderson to Jeannette Foster

Chalet Rose, Avenue Victoria
Le Cannet (A.M.) France
May 28, 1960

Dear Mrs. [sic] Foster,

I have come upon your book belatedly, but have been much interested in it, and have wondered if *you* might not be interested in reading a story I wrote two years ago on the subject of variance. All books on lesbianism seem to be written from a negative point of view; my idea, in telling a true story, was that the positive point of view is more enlightening.

My Paris agent was convinced that a French publisher would take it immediately, but she was overly optimistic — no one wanted it, not even the Olympia Press.

Ben Hecht has been trying for a year to place the ms., without results so far. All of which suggests to me that you may know of some more private publishing house that would find it interesting as case history and be willing to bring it out in a limited edition.

In any case, I shall be enormously grateful if you will give me your opinion. Being in France, I can't send stamps for the return of the ms., so I am taking the liberty of enclosing a dollar for postage. Do please forgive the rather battered. ms. — Ben Hecht has the original.

With my thanks for the pleasure I've had in reading your very illuminating book,

Cordially yours,
[signed] Margaret Anderson

In case my name is unfamiliar to you, I founded *The Little Review* in 1914 and introduced the world to the creative writers of the twenties — Joyce, Eliot, Pound, Hemingway and all the others. Our publication of Joyce's "Ulysses" was a *cause célèbre* — we were fined and finger-printed for publishing "obscene literature."

Jeannette Foster to Margaret Anderson

4346 Harrison Street
Kansas City 10, Missouri
June 8, 1960

Dear Miss Anderson,

Indeed your name is not unfamiliar to me, and I am much flattered that my book led you to communicate. During the years you were editing *The Little Review* in Chicago I was living there too — a bookishly precocious but timorous, impoverished and repressed little nonentity, enjoying a "nervous breakdown" due to scrapping my religion as a sixteen-year-old science major in 1913 and then in 1914 having the older woman I adored take off for four years of missionary teaching in China.

I remember well the Joyce uproar a little later, though the smoke had blown over by the time Robert Herrick mentioned it in his overcrowded Contemporary Lit course at the U. of Chicago. (By that time — 1920 — and I on my way to an M.A — the *cause célèbre* of the moment was *Jurgen,* and we all read Johnny Gunther's copy.) And there *you,* all that time, publishing people with whom I was filling my bookshelves five to a dozen years later — Dorothy Richardson, Ezra Pound, F.M. Ford, Djuna Barnes, Aldous Huxley and the rest. . . . I also recall dimly the echoes of *My Thirty Years' War,* though I didn't read it at the time, being involved in a crisis of my own. (I looked up the Sherwood Anderson eulogy in the yellowed pages of *New Republic* for 1930 yesterday; *very* satisfying.) I did come near buying *Fiery Fountains* in 1951, suspecting that the friendship described was "variant" if not more explicit; but knowing that no printable autobiography would really admit such a thing, and as I was holding my Opus down to a length anyone would ever consent to print, I left buying it till it appeared on a Used Books list last spring. And then immediately we sold our house and I had to· pack all my books for a year's storage, and so I have the reading of it still to look forward to. But I have suspected that Mlle. Leblanc may be the "Claire" of *Forbidden Fires?*

But you did not ask for a chapter of *my* autobiography. You want a publisher. If only I knew of one, two lesbian novels and three novelle of my own would be in print. And frankly, I fear you have even less chance than I of "making it," because your work is so far superior. You have the real "matter" which differentiates excellence from mere slick readability. (I am unable to be luridly sensational in the current Paper-Back-Original manner.) So you have not only the lesbian element for handicap. And who, I ask you, would in this Publishing-as-Big-Business decade risk printing Henry James or Virginia Woolf if they were newcomers, or Dorothy Richardson at any price? *We,* alas, are badly out of date.

So the answer is "vanity" (I stubbornly call it "subsidy") publishing. But don't, oh DO NOT, enter into any deal with Vantage Press! (You got their name correct on both letters; they pasted a new address slip onto the MS package so I cannot tell about that; you slipped into "Vanguard" only in the text of your first letter.) Here are the reasons My book was refused by six or seven university presses, though Rutgers kept it seven months before a new Director reversed the interim staff's decision to use it. I then tried Pageant Press (101 Fifth Ave., N.Y.), whose really gentlemanly editor showed interest and understanding — and made me a price of $6,200. As that was considerably more than a year's salary, I felt I could not afford it, though their work compares favorably with that of any university press.

I then fell for Vantage's price of $4,450 — *and* the statistical evidence in *Publishers Weekly* that in 1954 their volume of output was second (or third?) largest in the U.S. (At that time the F.T.C. hadn't started its exposé of the subsidy houses.) I read my 25- or 26-clause contract with minutest care, questioned several points, and had adequate answers in writing.

What in my naiveté I never suspected of being the booby-trap was the clause specifying that the author would accept all editorial corrections. I thought that would relieve me of the agony of vetting the whole 400+ pages for inconsistencies of capitalization, punctuation et al.

Now, I taught college English for nine years, and for eleven (in library schools) the writing of book reviews and annotations. So I rather liked my own prose style in the Opus. Fancy, then, receiving galley proof in which an obvious semi-literate had been turned loose to revise and shorten about 10% of my sentences, leaving many of the truncated bits downright ungrammatical! I changed them all right back. Then I refused to have the book jacket one of the those newsstand come-hither nude jobs that Vantage thought would "sell." And I screamed until I got proofs of my bibliography (which they didn't intend to provide), those being absolutely imperative before I could check notes and index (which I had to do myself) against them.

As a total result, I was billed for better than $1100 for "author's changes," besides a $350 legal fee for judging the text safe from libel suits. (As if I hadn't had a weather eye out for that in every sentence I wrote. I had even corresponded with Natalie Clifford Barney, bless her, about my section *re* her and Renée Vivien.)

So . . . Vantage sold ca. 550 copies before they declared the volume too slow-moving to retain "in print." And I have not only not received one cent of royalties, but on paper they claim I still owe them money. The best copyright-law firm in Missouri says to ignore the claim; but they also say I couldn't win a suit save by going to N.Y.C. to wage it, and if I did win, costs would exceed winnings.

The one good subsidy house beside Pageant (I mean the F.T.C. hasn't had them in court for malpractice according to *Publishers Weekly*) is Exposition Press (380 Park Ave. South, N.Y. 16). The publisher, Edward Uhlan, in his autobiographical *Rogue of Publishers' Row*, 1956, claims the longest record in the subsidy business (two decades), and no jail sentences! The third possibility, though I fear there would be no money in it and no recognition by reviewers (— but then, review sheets consistently and purposely ignore subsidized titles too —) is to give your MS to one of the three groups of organized homosexuals on the Pacific coast. They put out volumes in various qualities of multigraphing, and have incorporated book-selling services; advertising is run in little mags published by all three.

They are: Daughters of Bilitis (lesbian); Pres. Del Martin, 165 O'Farrell Street, San Francisco. Mag: *The Ladder.* / The Mattachine Society (male). Pres. Harold Call, 693 Mission Street, San Francisco. They operate the Pan-Graphic Press and issue (besides a *Mattachine Review* for members) a *Dorian Book Quarterly.* / One, Inc., Los Angeles, Cal. Mag: *One,* allegedly for both sexes, but preponderantly male rather than lesbian emphasis, both in membership and published material. None of these groups, I regret to say, are intellectuals primarily. They are crusaders for social recognition of the homosexual; and since, along with my remote-control friend, Mary Renault, I "don't want to opt myself out of the human race", I have refused to attend their conventions or moderate their panels. But if they are the only way to get into print, I'll take that way. My own MSS are not with any one of them right now simply because a "do-less" agent in NY has had them for months, and I cannot risk prying them loose from him until I am sure of being at one address for some length of time. (I am *here* until I retire from my job as Reference Librarian at U.K.C. on July 29.) I expect you will want the copy I have of *Forbidden Fires* returned to you rather than sent to any of the Pacific groups direct. Then you can do as you choose about which copy and which group.

And now that, as one may say, the board is cleared of business, I should like to return to *Forbidden Fires.* (A perfect "selling title," according to my experience of the paperback-originals on the newsstands — in whose company, however, you would hardly care to have it found.) It is a really beautiful thing, not only in form but in almost every word of its phrasing. I am of an age to have been steeped in Romantic Love myself; you capture its essence to perfection, as also the truth that it can survive long only through unfulfillment, whether through separation or imposed "restriction." The six years of my life (age 28–34) that most nearly duplicate your experience were spent (as faculty) in a southern college dormitory, in daily proximity to a charmer as skilled as your Audrey, but whose reason for maintaining distance was that I "didn't know what she wanted and there were plenty of these college kids who did. She'd never *taught* anybody a thing." She boasted of many overt affairs with girls and women of all ages, but would not allow the words "homosexual" or "lesbian" to be uttered in her presence. How do minds get twisted into such incredibly contradictory patterns? Probably through such complete lack of logical intellectual training that there is nothing there that *we* could call "mind". Only verbalized emoting. Oh, that "Oxford Group" scene of yours! God, have I been there! *My* gal was a Southern Baptist, and sang two or three times a week in church. But she had no more real religion than a blue-eyed white kitten (or maybe a green-eyed black witch's "familiar").

Needless to say, my Hannis was a really great beauty — her photograph still draws strangers hypnotically across a room — and was possessed of consummate physical grace and magnetism; had a singing voice indistinguishable from victrola records of Rosa Ponselle — and did she know how to use it!!

Well — I fear it is time to check this outpouring and send this missive on its way. Thank you again for writing to me, and I dearly hope we shall both get into print one way or another before many moons have waned!

I can scarcely wait to retire at the end of July and begin savoring life as it hourly passes. This diabolic age of rush, "status seekers," automotive engine exhaust and noise by land or by air, and no time for charm!

For your letter *mille grazia* —

[Signed] (*Miss*) Jeannette Foster

Bibliography

1. Works Written or Edited by Margaret Anderson (1886–1973)

[editor] *The Little Review*. Chicago, New York and Paris, 1914–1929.
My Thirty Years' War. New York: Covici Friede, 1930; 2nd ed., New York: Horizon Press, 1969.
The Fiery Fountains. New York: Hermitage House, 1951; 2nd ed., New York: Horizon Press, 1969.
[editor] *The Little Review Anthology*. New York: Hermitage House, 1953.
The Unknowable Gurdjieff. London: Routledge and Kegan Paul, 1962; reprint, New York: Samuel Weiser, 1973.
The Strange Necessity. New York: Horizon Press, 1969.

2. Select Bibliography

Benstock, Shari. *Women of the Left Bank: Paris 1910–1940*. Austin, Texas: U.niv. of Texas Press, 1986.
Broe, Mary Lynn. *Women's Writing in Exile: Alien and Critical*. Chapel Hill: Univ. of North Carolina Press, 1989.
Bryer, Jackson R. "'A Trial-Track for Racers': Margaret Anderson and *The Little Review*. Ph.D. dissertation, University of Wisconsin, 1965.
Ford, Hugh. *Four Lives in Paris*. San Francisco: North Point Press, 1987.
Foster, Jeannette H. *Sex Variant Women in Literature*. London: Frederick Muller, 1958.
Gelernter, David. *1939: The Lost World of the Fair*. New York: The Free Press, 1995.
[Grier, Barbara.] Gene Damon, ed. *The Ladder*, 1956–1972.
Gurdjieff, G. I. *Meetings with Remarkable Men*. New York: E. P. Dutton, 1969.
Harris, Bertha. "The More Profound Nationality of Their Lesbianism: Lesbian Society in Paris in the 1920's," in *Amazon Expedition*, edited by Phyllis Birkby et al. New York: Times Change Press, 1973.

Hills, Mathilda. "Margaret Anderson" in *Notable American Women: The Modern Period,* edited by Barbara Sicherman et al. Cambridge, Mass: Harvard Univ. Press, 1980.

Hulme, Kathryn C. *Undiscovered Country.* Boston: Little, Brown, 1966.

Kazin, Alfred. "A Life Led as a Work of Art." *The New York Times Book Review,* 16 August 1970.

Kennedy, J. Gerald. *Imagining Paris: Exile, Writing, and American Identity.* New Haven: Yale Univ. Press, 1993.

Knapp, Bettina. *Maurice Maeterlinck.* Boston: Twayne Publishers, G. K. Hall, 1975.

Krafft-Ebing, Richard von. *Psychopathia Sexualis,* adapted from the 12th German edition by F. J. Rebman. New York: Rebman, 1906.

Leblanc, Georgette. *Souvenirs: My Life with Maeterlinck,* trans. Janet Flanner. New York: E. P. Dutton, 1932.

————. *La Machine à Courage.* Paris: J. B. Janin, 1947.

Peters, Fritz. *Gurdjieff Remembered.* London: Victor Gollancz, 1965.

Rule, Jane. *Lesbian Images.* Garden City, N.Y.: Doubleday, 1975.

Scott, Thomas L., et al., eds. *The Letters of Ezra Pound to Margaret Anderson: "The Little Review" Correspondence.* New York: New Directions, 1988.

Smith, Sidonie. *A Poetics of Women's Autobiography: Marginality and the Fictions of Self-Representation.* Bloomington: Indiana Univ. Press, 1987.

Solano, Solita. *This Way Up.* New York: G. P. Putnam's Sons, 1927.

————. *Statue in a Field.* Paris: privately printed, 1935.

————. "The Hotel Napoleon Bonaparte" in *Quarterly Journal of the Library of Congress,* Vol. 34, No. 4 (Oct. 1977), 308–13.

Webb, James. *The Harmonious Circle.* New York: G. P. Putnam's Sons, 1980.

Weinstein, Wendy. *Beyond Imagining.* Videocassette. New York: Women Make Movies, 1992.

Wineapple, Brenda. *Genêt: A Biography of Janet Flanner.* New York: Ticknor & Fields, 1989.

FORBIDDEN FIRES by Margaret C. Anderson. Edited by Mathilda Hills. 176 pp. Famous author's "unpublished" Lesbian romance.
ISBN 1-56280-123-6 $21.95

SIDE TRACKS by Teresa Stores. 288 pp. Gender-bending Lesbians on the road.   ISBN 1-56280-122-8   10.95

HOODED MURDER by Annette Van Dyke. 176 pp. 1st Jessie Batelle Mystery.   ISBN 1-56280-134-1   10.95

WILDWOOD FLOWERS by Julia Watts. 208 pp. Hilarious and heart-warming tale of true love.   ISBN 1-56280-127-9   10.95

NEVER SAY NEVER by Linda Hill. 224 pp. Rule #1: Never get involved with . . .   ISBN 1-56280-126-0   10.95

THE SEARCH by Melanie McAllester. 240 pp. Exciting top cop Tenny Mendoza case.   ISBN 1-56280-150-3   10.95

THE WISH LIST by Saxon Bennett. 192 pp. Romance through the years.   ISBN 1-56280-125-2   10.95

FIRST IMPRESSIONS by Kate Calloway. 208 pp. P.I. Cassidy James' first case.   ISBN 1-56280-133-3   10.95

OUT OF THE NIGHT by Kris Bruyer. 192 pp. Spine-tingling thriller.   ISBN 1-56280-120-1   10.95

NORTHERN BLUE by Tracey Richardson. 224 pp. Police recruits Miki & Miranda — passion in the line of fire.   ISBN 1-56280-118-X   10.95

LOVE'S HARVEST by Peggy Herring. 176 pp. by the author of *Once More With Feeling.*   ISBN 1-56280-117-1   10.95

THE COLOR OF WINTER by Lisa Shapiro. 208 pp. Romantic love beyond your wildest dreams.   ISBN 1-56280-116-3   10.95

FAMILY SECRETS by Laura DeHart Young. 208 pp. Enthralling romance and suspense.   ISBN 1-56280-119-8   10.95

INLAND PASSAGE by Jane Rule. 288 pp. Tales exploring conventional & unconventional relationships.   ISBN 0-930044-56-8   10.95

DOUBLE BLUFF by Claire McNab. 208 pp. 7th Detective Carol Ashton Mystery.   ISBN 1-56280-096-5   10.95

BAR GIRLS by Lauran Hoffman. 176 pp. See the movie, read
the book! ISBN 1-56280-115-5   10.95

THE FIRST TIME EVER edited by Barbara Grier & Christine
Cassidy. 272 pp. Love stories by Naiad Press authors.
ISBN 1-56280-086-8   14.95

MISS PETTIBONE AND MISS McGRAW by Brenda Weathers.
208 pp. A charming ghostly love story. ISBN 1-56280-151-1   10.95

CHANGES by Jackie Calhoun. 208 pp. Involved romance and
relationships. ISBN 1-56280-083-3   10.95

FAIR PLAY by Rose Beecham. 256 pp. 3rd Amanda Valentine
Mystery. ISBN 1-56280-081-7   10.95

PAXTON COURT by Diane Salvatore. 256 pp. Erotic and wickedly
funny contemporary tale about the business of learning to live
together. ISBN 1-56280-109-0   21.95

PAYBACK by Celia Cohen. 176 pp. A gripping thriller of romance,
revenge and betrayal. ISBN 1-56280-084-1   10.95

THE BEACH AFFAIR by Barbara Johnson. 224 pp. Sizzling
summer romance/mystery/intrigue. ISBN 1-56280-090-6   10.95

GETTING THERE by Robbi Sommers. 192 pp. Nobody does it
like Robbi! ISBN 1-56280-099-X   10.95

FINAL CUT by Lisa Haddock. 208 pp. 2nd Carmen Ramirez
Mystery. ISBN 1-56280-088-4   10.95

FLASHPOINT by Katherine V. Forrest. 256 pp. A Lesbian
blockbuster! ISBN 1-56280-079-5   10.95

CLAIRE OF THE MOON by Nicole Conn. Audio Book —Read
by Marianne Hyatt. ISBN 1-56280-113-9   16.95

FOR LOVE AND FOR LIFE: INTIMATE PORTRAITS OF
LESBIAN COUPLES by Susan Johnson. 224 pp.
ISBN 1-56280-091-4   14.95

DEVOTION by Mindy Kaplan. 192 pp. See the movie — read
the book! ISBN 1-56280-093-0   10.95

SOMEONE TO WATCH by Jaye Maiman. 272 pp. 4th Robin
Miller Mystery. ISBN 1-56280-095-7   10.95

GREENER THAN GRASS by Jennifer Fulton. 208 pp. A young
woman — a stranger in her bed. ISBN 1-56280-092-2   10.95

TRAVELS WITH DIANA HUNTER by Regine Sands. Erotic
lesbian romp. Audio Book (2 cassettes) ISBN 1-56280-107-4   16.95

CABIN FEVER by Carol Schmidt. 256 pp. Sizzling suspense
and passion. ISBN 1-56280-089-1   10.95

THERE WILL BE NO GOODBYES by Laura DeHart Young. 192
pp. Romantic love, strength, and friendship. ISBN 1-56280-103-1   10.95

FAULTLINE by Sheila Ortiz Taylor. 144 pp. Joyous comic
lesbian novel. ISBN 1-56280-108-2   9.95

OPEN HOUSE by Pat Welch. 176 pp. 4th Helen Black Mystery.
ISBN 1-56280-102-3   10.95

ONCE MORE WITH FEELING by Peggy J. Herring. 240 pp.
Lighthearted, loving romantic adventure. ISBN 1-56280-089-2   10.95

FOREVER by Evelyn Kennedy. 224 pp. Passionate romance — love
overcoming all obstacles. ISBN 1-56280-094-9   10.95

WHISPERS by Kris Bruyer. 176 pp. Romantic ghost story
ISBN 1-56280-082-5   10.95

NIGHT SONGS by Penny Mickelbury. 224 pp. 2nd Gianna Maglione
Mystery. ISBN 1-56280-097-3   10.95

GETTING TO THE POINT by Teresa Stores. 256 pp. Classic
southern Lesbian novel. ISBN 1-56280-100-7   10.95

PAINTED MOON by Karin Kallmaker. 224 pp. Delicious
Kallmaker romance. ISBN 1-56280-075-2   10.95

THE MYSTERIOUS NAIAD edited by Katherine V. Forrest &
Barbara Grier. 320 pp. Love stories by Naiad Press authors.
ISBN 1-56280-074-4   14.95

DAUGHTERS OF A CORAL DAWN by Katherine V. Forrest.
240 pp. Tenth Anniversay Edition. ISBN 1-56280-104-X   10.95

BODY GUARD by Claire McNab. 208 pp. 6th Carol Ashton
Mystery. ISBN 1-56280-073-6   10.95

CACTUS LOVE by Lee Lynch. 192 pp. Stories by the beloved
storyteller. ISBN 1-56280-071-X   9.95

SECOND GUESS by Rose Beecham. 216 pp. 2nd Amanda Valentine
Mystery. ISBN 1-56280-069-8   9.95

THE SURE THING by Melissa Hartman. 208 pp. L.A. earthquake
romance. ISBN 1-56280-078-7   9.95

A RAGE OF MAIDENS by Lauren Wright Douglas. 240 pp. 6th Caitlin
Reece Mystery. ISBN 1-56280-068-X   10.95

TRIPLE EXPOSURE by Jackie Calhoun. 224 pp. Romantic drama
involving many characters. ISBN 1-56280-067-1   9.95

UP, UP AND AWAY by Catherine Ennis. 192 pp. Delightful
romance. ISBN 1-56280-065-5   9.95

PERSONAL ADS by Robbi Sommers. 176 pp. Sizzling short
stories. ISBN 1-56280-059-0   9.95

FLASHPOINT by Katherine V. Forrest. 256 pp. Lesbian
blockbuster! ISBN 1-56280-043-4   22.95

CROSSWORDS by Penny Sumner. 256 pp. 2nd Victoria Cross
Mystery. ISBN 1-56280-064-7   9.95

SWEET CHERRY WINE by Carol Schmidt. 224 pp. A novel of
suspense.   ISBN 1-56280-063-9   9.95
CERTAIN SMILES by Dorothy Tell. 160 pp. Erotic short stories.
                                             ISBN 1-56280-066-3   9.95
EDITED OUT by Lisa Haddock. 224 pp. 1st Carmen Ramirez
Mystery.   ISBN 1-56280-077-9   9.95
WEDNESDAY NIGHTS by Camarin Grae. 288 pp. Sexy
adventure.   ISBN 1-56280-060-4   10.95
SMOKEY O by Celia Cohen. 176 pp. Relationships on the
playing field.   ISBN 1-56280-057-4   9.95
KATHLEEN O'DONALD by Penny Hayes. 256 pp. Rose and
Kathleen find each other and employment in 1909 NYC.
                                             ISBN 1-56280-070-1   9.95
STAYING HOME by Elisabeth Nonas. 256 pp. Molly and Alix
want a baby . . . or do they?   ISBN 1-56280-076-0   10.95
TRUE LOVE by Jennifer Fulton. 240 pp. Six lesbians searching
for love in all the "right" places.   ISBN 1-56280-035-3   10.95
GARDENIAS WHERE THERE ARE NONE by Molleen Zanger.
176 pp. Why is Melanie inextricably drawn to the old house?
                                             ISBN 1-56280-056-6   9.95
KEEPING SECRETS by Penny Mickelbury. 208 pp. 1st Gianna
Maglione Mystery.   ISBN 1-56280-052-3   9.95
THE ROMANTIC NAIAD edited by Katherine V. Forrest &
Barbara Grier. 336 pp. Love stories by Naiad Press authors.
                                             ISBN 1-56280-054-X   14.95
UNDER MY SKIN by Jaye Maiman. 336 pp. 3rd Robin Miller
Mystery.   ISBN 1-56280-049-3.   10.95
STAY TOONED by Rhonda Dicksion. 144 pp. Cartoons — 1st
collection since *Lesbian Survival Manual.*   ISBN 1-56280-045-0   9.95
CAR POOL by Karin Kallmaker. 272pp. Lesbians on wheels
and then some!   ISBN 1-56280-048-5   10.95
NOT TELLING MOTHER: STORIES FROM A LIFE by Diane
Salvatore. 176 pp. Her 3rd novel.   ISBN 1-56280-044-2   9.95
GOBLIN MARKET by Lauren Wright Douglas. 240pp. 5th Caitlin
Reece Mystery.   ISBN 1-56280-047-7   10.95

These are just a few of the many Naiad Press titles — we are the oldest an
largest lesbian/feminist publishing company in the world. Please request
complete catalog. We offer personal service; we encourage and welcom
direct mail orders from individuals who have limited access to bookstore
carrying our publications.